eternal HEAT

THE FIREWORK GIRLS

JORDYN WHITE

LARGE PRINT EDITION

Published by Velvet Pen Books
United States of America

www.jordynwhitebooks.com

ISBN 978-1-945261-44-2

Printed in the USA

Cover Design: Letitia Hasser | RBA Designs

Books by Jordyn White
Available in Large Print:

Firework Girls Series

Forbidden Heat

Midnight Heat

Eternal Heat

Nuclear Heat

Holiday Heat

Beautiful Rivers Series

Beautiful Mine

Beautiful Fall

Beautiful Dark

Beautiful Deep

Hearts on Fire Series

Heart of Glass

Eternal Heat

Chapter 1

I'm only moments away from laying eyes on the lifelong dream that never happened.

We're on day four of our Firework Girls trip to New York City, and crossing the famous plaza in front of Lincoln Center. When Isabella asked for our number one "must-do" item for this trip, that's what I said: Lincoln Center. But I was being kind of sneaky, because what I really want to see is across the street.

In the center of the plaza is a large, flat reflection pool with a stone, abstract sculpture in the center. Lincoln Center is on the other side of the pool, and in front of us is the large area known as Illumination Lawn. Not like any kind of lawn I've ever seen, this is a grass-covered steel platform that starts at ground level, then rises toward the back. It's something only New Yorkers could define (and use) as a lawn.

Past the lawn, I get my first glimpse of the multi-storied white building across the street.

Chloe's been focused on the refection pool, but when she notices Illumination Lawn, she bounds ahead. "Cool!"

Her auburn-hair flowing behind her, Chloe reaches the grassy steps of the lawn and leads the way to the top. This suits me fine. The rear of the raised lawn will give an excellent view.

We walk up the grass and approach the back railing. The sidewalk and street are below. Across the street the white building stretches along almost the entire block opposite us. In simple, unassuming type, the lettering on the building reads: "The Juilliard School."

"Are you sure this isn't too high for you, Sam?" Chloe asks. "Do you want to wait at the bottom?"

"Shut it, Chloe," Sam says easily, rolling her eyes. When Chloe had declared her "must do" item the Empire State Building, Sam had practically disowned her. She's a teeny bit afraid of heights, that one. We didn't try to push her to go to the top with us (as if anyone could get Sam to do what she doesn't want to do anyway), but we're entitled to a good-natured jab every now and then.

I'm too distracted to join in their teasing. There's The Juilliard School. Right freaking there!

"Leave her alone," Isabella says, leaning on the rail and looking like a tall, brown Greek goddess. "She can't help that she's not used to heights, being so bitty all her life."

"Har, har," Sam says. She's just barely 5'4" and her blonde hair is short and wild, just like she is.

That's all right. I have enough hair for both of us. Mine's blonde as well, but it hangs past my waist even when it's in a braid, which it usually is.

"This is why Ashley's my favorite," Sam says, hooking her arm through mine. "She doesn't tease me mercilessly."

"I'm your favorite because I'm the only one whose activities for the day are all on the ground," I retort.

3

"That's true," Sam agrees, sticking her tongue out at Isabella.

Isabella's must-do item is Ellis Island—where her family came to America from Italy and Greece back in the 1960s—and the Statue of Liberty. That's not on our itinerary for two more days but I already know there's no way is Sam going to the top of our Lady of Liberty either.

I put my hand on the rear railing of the lawn and take it all in. The Juilliard School stretches to the right. At the corner is the unique, angled entryway I've seen so many times in pictures.

My eyes return to the quietly-assured text opposite us—The Juilliard School—and I exhale with wonder, unable to hide it. Time to come clean. "This is what I've wanted to see all day."

"Juilliard?" Chloe asks and I nod.

"That makes sense." Isabella is pretty smart, being a Harvard grad student and all. But though she might think she knows why I'd want to see this school, she doesn't. I'm not about to correct her.

"For the top school in music, it's not as pretty as I would have thought." Sam cocks her head at it.

She's the only one here who knows I once applied to Juilliard. In fact, she's the only one who knows everything Juilliard represents to me.

And who.

I'd like to say I haven't thought about him in years, but it'd be a lie.

"Well, there's some debate about which school really ranks at the top," I admit, "but Juilliard is a legend like no other. There's no denying that."

"Hartman's right up there," Sam says firmly. "It's a great school." The other two nod in agreement.

I smile. These girls always have my back.

Hartman College, where we all met as undergrads and where I'm about to start my second year in their Master's program, does in fact have a highly-regarded music conservatory that makes pretty much every "best of" list Juilliard does.

But none of that changes the fact that, in my eyes, The Juilliard School is practically glittering in the sun over there, right along with the lucky students entering and exiting the building like they belong there. Which, of course, they do. But even though Hartman has a stellar program that I'm glad to be part of (truly), it's located an hour-and-a-half inland from the central Californian coast and not right smack dab in the middle of the classical music capital of America.

Then there's the other thing.

I imagine him walking into the building, walking the halls, laughing with friends. He's probably had girls, too.

My heart clenches at the thought, in spite of myself.

Maybe it wasn't such a good idea coming here. The sting of it all is sharper than I anticipated. I kind of thought I was over it enough. It's been five years, after all.

But as I stand here on Illumination Lawn, gaze on the celebrated school that is Juilliard, and think about the person it represents, my heart can't help but wonder...

What if?

School's been back in session for a mere three days when I walk into Kopp Hall, one of Hartman's smaller auditoriums used for rehearsals and recitals. Today is the pre-audition for an upcoming regional competition, which the department heads emailed everyone about a week ago. There's an atmosphere of slightly organized chaos. Students from all across the musical disciplines are scattered about in the seats, plugging up the aisles, lingering just off stage. The quiet hum of multiple conversations lingers in the air.

On stage is a black grand piano, currently unoccupied, and a few scattered music stands and plastic chairs. A small table is off to the side, where a grad student is sitting with a stack of packets. Currently a girl is hauling her cello onstage from the wings; it's almost as big as she is.

About ten rows back from stage are the judges. As I make my way down one of the aisles to find a seat, I crane my neck to see who they are.

There are three judges, including Professor Reinecht. He discussed the auditions in class yesterday. Not all competitions involve the sort of semi-informal screening process this one does, but even so, for many of Hartman's musicians, today is only a technicality. It's a way for the department heads to screen new students and check our selections to make sure Hartman is well represented

"Nothing for you to worry about," he told me yesterday.

I'm in that weird state of mind where I'm both worried and not worried. While the competition itself will be fierce, I'm not worried about qualifying at this pre-audition level. Last year I made it through both formal rounds of the competition itself, and placed first in my category and third overall. It wasn't a bad way to start off my graduate career, I have to admit. The prize money helped with living expenses for a while too, and even gave me enough to add a sizeable chunk to my piano savings fund.

On the other hand, you can never take anything for granted in the music world. The reality is, those three judges up there have the authority to tell me or anyone we're out.

I pick a row and scoot down to sit next to Toshiko, a fellow second-year grad student. He's wearing his trademark Hawaiian shorts and Birkenstocks. His violin case is in the seat next to him but his violin is on his lap, ready to go. He spots me coming and moves his case to the seat on his other side. We smile and wave at each other in acknowledgement, but don't say anything because one of the judges has banged the gavel to indicate the next audition is beginning.

The conversations in the hall cease immediately. I settle into my seat as the deep vibrato of the cello on stage fills the hall. I don't recognize the player, so I assume she must be a first-year grad student. At the conclusion of her piece, the judges give their remarks in turn. Two of them express some concerns and my heart clenches as she's told she's not quite ready for this one. I've seen this happen before, but it's a bit unsettling when it's the first audition I see.

The low sound of conversations starts up again as the cellist gathers her music and instrument, trying to maintain her composure. Poor thing.

Toshiko fidgets with the folder on his lap. "What are you playing?" I ask.

He names a concerto by Haydn and I nod with approval.

"You?"

"Paganini Etude Number 6 by Liszt." He doesn't ask where my music is. He knows me well enough to know I have it memorized. "Which time slot are you in?" I ask.

"Ten to noon. Naturally I'm near the end."

My slot is noon to two and it's nearly noon now. "You've gotta be next, or close to it. Unless they're running behind."

We hear one of the judges call Toshiko's name into the microphone.

"At laaaast!" he sings sarcastically, taking his violin and music with him as he works down the row.

"Good luck!"

I listen to his piece and the judges' comments—they love him of course, no surprise there—and watch as he goes to the little table on stage to get his packet. I settle in, prepared for a wait. I pull out my phone and start scrolling through my feed on Instagram. Toshiko comes down our row, returns to his case, and starts putting away his instrument. I glance up and give him a smile. "Nicely done."

"Thanks."

Professor Reinecht calls out the next name and I think I'm hearing things.

I drop my hands to my lap and sit up straighter. "Who did he just say?"

A mere six rows in front of me, and off to the right, he stands. Oh my god. Then Toshiko says the name of the man I once knew so long ago: "They said Erik Williams."

It's a little like being in the Twilight Zone. Erik doesn't belong here at Hartman, with Toshiko saying his name like it's the most normal thing in the world. Erik belongs in a grand house by the river in a whole different world.

But there he is, climbing the steps to the stage. Just like that.

My skin crawls and my heart pounds in this sickening way. I sink lower in my chair, but my eyes follow his every move. He looks the same, but different. He's just as handsome as ever, maybe even more so if that's possible, but he's broader in the chest and his hair is a bit longer and he's sporting a five o'clock shadow. He's wearing black jeans and a casual button-down shirt with the sleeves rolled up past his elbows.

I know those forearms and those hands. I know those long fingers. Down to the last detail, I remember it all.

As he settles himself on the bench and lays out his sheet music, I'm struck by his impossible good looks. Men this handsome aren't exactly what you'd consider typical fare anywhere, but definitely not among the world of classical pianists. He looks more like a rock star.

Maybe that's why, in the midst of the shock and pain and (yes) anger at seeing him again, my heart is still fluttering in that maddening way. Still. After all this time. After everything.

Then he begins to play.

Like the rest of him, his music is deeply familiar to me, but it too has changed. It's more mature. More controlled. In fact, it's absolutely heartbreaking. That deep, haunting quality to his music is still there. Its ability to render me helpless hasn't lessened at all.

Oh, how I remember this.

What happened all those years ago has never truly left me, but seeing him and listening to him brings it all back with such freshness, I don't know whether to cry or laugh or rage. I'm flooded with so many memories, all wrapped up in the sweet torture of his music. I'm too stunned to do more than stare. I can barely breathe.

By the time he's finished and the judges are giving him their praises (of course, of course), my brain kicks into a different gear. I realize Toshiko is gone, though I don't know if he said goodbye or if I acknowledged his departure. It takes about two seconds for me to realize Erik is a

13

student here, to wonder why in the hell that is, and to comprehend that he's now my competition, which is a completely different sort of problem.

In the next second I've sunk even lower in my seat and decided I'm going to just hide until he leaves and then come up with a plan to make sure we never see each other ever again until I get my degree and can get the heck out of here.

A tiny part of my brain realizes that's not the kind of thing that can actually happen, but that's not the part in charge right now.

My eyes are glued to him as he crosses the stage and picks up his packet. Before he even gets to the steps my plan is blown out of the water.

"Ashley Morrison," Professor Reinecht calls.

My heart stops. Erik freezes, a look of shock registering on his face. He immediately starts to scan the audience.

Oh god.

Seconds pass and neither one of us moves. He hasn't spotted me yet. I want him to just go. But then Professor Reinecht calls out my name more forcefully and obedience brings me shakily to my feet.

That's when he sees me. For the first time in five years, my eyes meet the deep brown eyes of Erik Williams. My heart flips, as if it doesn't realize I'm not in love with Erik anymore. Could never be again.

My only consolation in this moment is he looks like he wants to run as much as I do.

Of course, that's the exact same thing that hurts.

I finally pull my eyes away. I focus on the ground in front of me as I sidestep down the row and to the aisle.

I glance at him, up ahead.

He's coming down from the stage one slow step at a time, and watching me with an expression of... what? Shock? Longing? Regret?

I pull my eyes from his, but as we continue to near one another, the sensations in my body ratchet up a notch. These sensations reach a frightening peak as we pass in the aisle—I'm careful not to touch or look at him—then decline again as we move farther away from each other. It's like my body is one giant Erik detector.

I grab the cold hand rail and concentrate on each step, certain I'll trip and fall if I don't. As I cross the stage—a stage I've been on a hundred times—it all feels so foreign to me, because I've never crossed this stage with Erik watching. Is he watching?

Without thinking, I glance toward the auditorium. My eyes find him immediately. He's standing in the aisle, and oh yes, he's watching me.

I turn away and focus on walking, a task which is suddenly more awkward and difficult than it should be. My body feels like butter.

I sit down on the edge of the bench. It's a bit too far away from the piano for comfort, but I'm too flustered to do anything about it. I bring my fingers to the keys out of habit, but I don't play. There's a sharp moment of panic when I remember why I'm here but can't remember what I'm playing.

Why didn't I bring my music? My hands hover over the keys, trembling. I wonder if the people in the audience can see it.

Then it comes back to me, <u>thank God</u>. Liszt. Yes, okay. I can do that.

I play a measure with rubbery fingers that race into the second measure with such clumsiness they trip all over each other.

I'm a trained musician. I know to keep going if I make a mistake. But this is so bad and I'm so shocked by the whole thing that I actually bring my fingers off the keys and clasp them in front of me.

This snaps me out of it. At least, out of it enough that I'm determined to play this piano like I actually know what the fuck I'm doing.

There's some murmuring in the audience. Professor Reinecht says, "What in the hell was that?"

He's not known for his subtlety.

"Sorry, I—"

"Start again. No more chances, Ashley."

"No, sir." No shit.

I take hold of myself and pull the bench up where it needs to be.

<u>Liszt,</u> I think forcefully, and begin to play.

It seems like an eternity, but I finally manage to get through my piece. I didn't make any obvious mistakes, but it definitely wasn't my best either. When I look up, I see Erik's back retreating out the auditorium door.

Oh, screw you.

"Well that was better, at least," Reinecht says tersely. He's no more happy about my performance than I am. Jesus, what a time for Erik Williams to show up!

The panel converses for a few seconds. They all nod and go back to their paperwork. Professor Reinecht leans into the microphone. "You're in. Get your packet and get off my stage."

Six Years Earlier

Chapter 2

As I walk along a branch of the Boise River, I can't believe I just got the first day of my senior year of high school under my belt. I still remember my first Monday as a nervous little freshman, walking those big halls and feeling so overwhelmed. Today, the other seniors and I were the ones strutting around like we own the place. The top class at last!

But it's a little intimidating, too. This time next year I'll be in college. It's crazy.

The path I'm on winds along the river, which is on my left. On my right is a line of fancy houses with impressive decks and patios, and perfectly landscaped backyards. The wrought-iron fencing allows people walking on the Greenbelt a perfect view of the privileged life of those who live here. This particular subdivision finally finished construction a few months ago. It's new enough that I haven't grown used to the presence of these houses, and my dad still complains about the consumption of the natural landscape thanks to the greed of the wealthy.

I don't know that I'm as bitter about it as he is. After all, even our rundown little house—in a neighborhood not terribly far from the river either—was an intruder on the landscape at some point. Granted, that was forty years ago. But still.

No, as I walk past one grand house after another, my reaction is more one of envy. I try not to feel that way, but I can't help it. Some of these houses are just so stunning. My favorites are the ones with huge bays of windows that give a broad view into the beautiful homes inside. I like to imagine being inside and wonder what it's like to have such a great view of the river every day.

Funny thing though, I almost never see anyone inside these homes. Where are they all the time, I wonder?

I come to the point where the river and the path curve off to the left, while a broad green area extends away to the right. More houses line the massive sculpted lawn as it retreats deeper into the new neighborhood. The lawn even boasts its own private pond. Just off the side of the public Greenbelt I'm walking along is an elegant-looking sign at the head the lawn that reads: "Private."

I always feel a bit of a twinge at this point, like I'm being excluded from the country club or something.

My steps don't slow however. This latter part of my walk is actually my favorite. There's a bridge up ahead that I like to stop on to enjoy the view.

Before I pass the private green area, however, I hear piano music that's so beautiful it stops me in my tracks. It reaches right into my chest and stops my heart, too. It must be coming from one of the homes lining the private lawn.

I hesitate.

Private.

But the music pulls my feet off the path and onto the private green. I walk slowly, glancing from one house to the next as I seek the source of the music. It's like I'm being led along by the Pied Piper.

Some five houses in is an elegant two-story with a wall of windows giving the inhabitants a view of the lawn and its broad private pond. Inside is a great room with a high ceiling, and to the rear is a gorgeous staircase leading up to the second floor landing. Other windows in the home give a glimpse into its modern kitchen and dining area, but I give this barely a glance.

In the living room is a gleaming black, grand piano, its raised lid currently blocking my view of the player. My steps slow even more. I continue until my view of the player is unobstructed.

I stop, stunned.

It's not an adult playing like that, it's a kid. He looks to be the same age I am. He's gorgeous too, I don't fail to notice that, but really it's the whole package that overwhelms me. Someone so young creating such a magical picture. Lord, that music.

It holds me in place until the song ends. Even the silence that follows is enhanced by the music I just heard. I let my breath out in a slow exhale. Who _is_ this boy?

He looks up and—since I'm directly in his line of sight—he looks right at me.

I startle and tuck my head down and hustle away. I'm too scared to look back to see if he's still watching me, but after passing a few more houses I realize I've gone deeper into the forbidden country club. I should've gone back to the Greenbelt.

I look back over my shoulder.

The line of houses is quiet. No movement. No sounds. No boy.

I stop and face toward the Greenbelt, clasping my hands in front of me. Okay, I'm just going to go back to the Greenbelt and go on my way.

I force myself to walk forward at a normal pace and try to look like I belong here. Me, in my cut-off shorts, flowing Bohemian shirt, and knit beanie. Yeah, I don't stick out at all.

When I get back to the house, the piano is empty. I'm disappointed—I wanted to hear more music—but I'm also nervous.

Where is he? I don't think I want him to see me again.

Do I?

I glance in the other windows. No one in the kitchen. No one in the great room or up on the landing.

The backyard, also vacant, is beautifully landscaped and has a few little nooks for sitting. The wooden patio deck runs almost the entire length of the house. There's an iron outdoor table set with thick cushions on the chairs. The yard and patio both have little decorations to give the whole thing a polished, rich look. Even these people's back yards are more decorated than my house.

On the right side of the patio is a French door leading into the house. My heart clenches as the door opens and out steps the boy, like he's looking for something. His eyes land on me and stay there, like I'm the one he was looking for.

I stop. I can't help it.

One corner of his mouth turns up in a half-smile. "Hi."

"Uh, hi."

He's wearing tan pants and a blue, collared shirt with a crest embroidered on the breast. I recognize it as the uniform for the private school so many of these rich kids attend.

"I was just listening to your music."

He smiles broader. It's a friendly smile and I start to unclench a bit.

"It was really good," I add.

"Thanks." He closes the door behind him and comes down the patio steps. I drift closer to the black, wrought iron fence that only comes to my waist. "Do you live around here?"

I have a fleeting thought that I'm about to get busted for being on private property, but I don't think he's going to care. "No. I'm over in Brookside. I was just walking along the Greenbelt when I heard you playing."

"I'm glad," he says. "I mean, that's cool."

He looks a little embarrassed and I smile. We both stop a few feet from the fence between us. "I'm Ashley, by the way."

"Erik." He steps forward and extends his hand to shake mine, just like a grown up.

I come closer and take his hand. I give him an awkward shake. I don't know why, but we both chuckle a bit.

"Do you play an instrument, Ashley?"

This question always makes me feel a little weird. "Uh, kind of. I guess."

"Oh yeah? Which one?"

Oh man. I should've just lied and said, No. "Uh..."

He smiles again. I like it. He's so cute. If he were a boy at my school, he's the kind of boy I would drool over in history class and admire from afar as he walks through the halls.

I realize I need to give an answer, so I finally confess, "Piano."

"Really?" His beautiful brown eyes light up. "How long have you been playing?"

I shrug. "I took a semester at the end of middle school, but they don't offer it at the high school."

"No private lessons?" he asks easily.

I shake my head. My parents could never afford private lessons. "Do you take lessons?" A stupid question, given the way he plays. I'd kill to play like that.

"Yeah. Since I was about six."

My eyebrows must've gone clear up into my hair. "No wonder you're so good. I just kind of watch YouTube videos and practice on the piano at school."

I'm actually surprised I admitted this, but I'm even more surprised how comfortable I feel admitting it.

"Don't you have a piano at home?"

I shake my head, but smile so he doesn't feel bad for me. Even if we had the money for a piano, we'd have nowhere to put it. Unless we got rid of my bed and put it in my room. I could sleep underneath it in a sleeping bag. That would be fine by me if it meant I could have access to a piano any old time I wanted instead of just an hour before and after school. Though, my parents did get me an electric keyboard for Christmas, which was just amazing. It's not the same, but it's not nothing.

There's a pause in the conversation as we consider each other. Erik gives me a tentative smile. "Wanna... come in and play a bit?"

I shouldn't. I don't know him. My parents wouldn't approve. But how can I say no? A cute boy has just asked me to come into his fancy house and play on his grand piano. My heart has a fluttery feeling in my chest. "As long as you agree to play more than I do. I'm not trained or anything."

"Agreed." He's smiling more broadly now and opening the back gate for me.

And just like that, I'm walking right into one of these beautiful yards and then, following his lead, right up the patio and to the backdoor.

He opens it but steps aside to let me go in first. I give him a tentative smile then go past him.

"Oh wow. How long is your hair?"

I'm wearing my blonde hair in double braids down to my waist.

"I mean..." He laughs nervously as I turn back to him. "Sorry, obviously I can see how long it is."

"Yeah, it's kinda long. I've worn it like this since I was a kid."

"It's pretty."

I feel my cheeks flush, but hope he doesn't notice.

"Come on," he says, smiling. He leads me into the living room.

His house is even more stunning on the inside than it was from the outside. I try not to gawk at the polished wood floors or the massive ceramic vases on the side table or the artwork I'm willing to bet didn't come from Target. There's a gorgeous living room set: a white couch and loveseat and two chairs. It all looks so fluffy and comfortable. And new and clean! We got our set from my grandma back when I was in elementary school. There are great big pink roses all over it and the arm of the loveseat is scratched up from the cat.

I follow Erik to the piano. We stop at the bench.

"Wanna go first?"

I shake my head emphatically.

He laughs and slides onto the bench. "Okay. What do you want to hear?"

I slowly come up to the piano and rest my hand on the smooth, shiny wood. <u>Oh, I just want to pet it!</u>

"Whatever you want." I take in the squat bookcase on the wall behind him. It's packed with music books.

"Well, how about Beethoven's Sonata in F? That was my recital piece last spring."

"Okay."

He puts his hands on the keys, but doesn't play. He looks at me. "You can sit if you want." I don't know if he means to sit on the bench or sit on the furniture. I would feel weird about either option.

"I'm okay."

"All right." Then he begins to play. It's just as good as the other piece I heard him play, and even more amazing because I'm right here next to it. The music reverberates through my body. I watch the hammers hopping against the strings. I watch his long fingers, dancing confidently along the keys. I watch his face. He's concentrating, eyes on his hands and not me. I slide my hand along the side of the piano some, now that he can't catch me doing it. God, this piano feels amazing!

I can't believe I'm standing here, in this house, listening to this music, and watching this boy play it. Oh, if only I'd been able to take lessons for as long as he has. Or any at all! But even if I had, I probably still wouldn't be able to play like this.

When he finishes his piece, I clap enthusiastically and he laughs.

"Thank you, thank you," he says in a mock serious voice and bows his head. "Your turn?"

He slides off the bench, so I can't very well say no. Oh well. What am I going to do about it? I may as well do what I can.

I decide to play one of my favorite songs. It's not classical, but it has an engaging, confident feel I could use right now.

"Okay. I'll play the Overture Theme from Phantom of the Opera."

He raises his eyebrows and nods his head. "Nice."

"We'll see if you think so after I play it. Just remember, I'm not trained."

"It's okay. We're just having fun, right?"

I look up at him and he's giving me a genuine smile. My heart does a little flip flop and I smile back.

I look back at the keyboard, which is considerably longer than the one at school. I want to touch every key. Instead I take a resolute breath and start to play.

I don't usually play in front of people, so I'm surprised when I slide deep down into the music just like I do when I'm alone. The fancy house I'm in disappears. Cute, cute Erik disappears. It's only me and my music, and the happiness of it swells inside me so big I let that spill over to what I'm playing.

This is what I love. This is what I love more than anything in the world, even more than my wonderful parents if I'm honest. That probably makes me a horrible, selfish person, but music is pure magic and belongs to a whole other world. Heaven itself, maybe. I can't help but give my complete devotion to it.

When I finish, my surroundings slowly come back to me and I realize I'm smiling. "Such a fun song." I grin up at my new friend. Even if I never see him again, we've shared music together so that makes us friends now. Not that I've ever had this experience before, but that's how it feels.

He's giving me a shrewd look. "You were pulling my leg!"

"Huh? About what?"

"No lessons my eye. Who's your teacher?"

I blink at him. "Just Mr. Bartlett in middle school."

He's still grinning, but he rolls his eyes. "Oh, come on. You can't play like that without taking lessons."

He's giving me a fluttery feeling in my chest again, but for completely different reasons now. "Was it okay?"

The grin slides off his face and now he's just staring at me wide-eyed. "You really, really never had lessons before?"

"Well, I practice. And I've watched just about every video you can on YouTube."

"That's... like... kind of amazing."

He drops onto the bench next to me. His elbow touches my bare arm for just a second and my heart beats a little faster. "What else can you play?"

But I don't answer. With him this close I'm aware of his body in a way I wasn't before. I realize I haven't seen or heard anyone else in the house. The combination makes me a little skittish. I'm not afraid of him, but my parents would not approve and I'm not sure how I feel about things either. "Are your parents home?"

"Nah. They work late." He says it matter-of-factly enough, but I sense something underneath. I wonder if he's like my friend, Jewel. Her mom is single and works two jobs and Jewel almost never sees her. She manages all right and everything, but she misses her mom sometimes, too.

My parents, on the other hand, are always there. I love them for that, even though it gets annoying at times. And speaking of them always being home, I'd better get going. If I hurry and head straight there, I may not be gone on my walk any more than I usually am. I don't really want to answer any questions.

"I'd better go." I stand and give him a grateful smile.

"Oh, okay..." He stands as well. "Thanks for coming in." He smiles back at me.

Is it just me or is he getting cuter and cuter? I realize I'm standing there smiling at him like an idiot, so I start to head for the door.

He comes with me. We leave his fantasy house and emerge onto the patio. "Are you sure you haven't had private lessons?"

"Nope." Maybe he's just flattering me, I don't know. But he seems sincere and I can't help but feel complimented.

"Well," he says as we cross the yard to the back gate, "your parents are wasting a great natural talent. They should sign you up."

"They want to, but we can't afford it." What the hell? I've already bared my soul by playing in front of him, I might as well show him the rest, too.

"Oh," he says awkwardly. "Sorry."

We stop by the gate. For the first time, I'm aware of the differences not just between our homes but between, probably, us. Here's this boy in his prep school uniform (which I'd managed to kind of forget about until now) and I'm in my ratty-but-oh-so-comfortable cut-offs and he's had years of private lessons while my parents can't even afford one.

"You don't need to be sorry. It is what it is. But they're really supportive and helped get the school to agree to let me use their piano before and after school."

He smiles and nods. "That's cool." I examine him for signs of pity, but find none.

"Well," he shrugs, "you could always come here, too."

I blink at him. He grins at me nervously.

"If you want."

The appeal of his invitation swells inside me like a bloom opening on a rose. Yes, I would like that very much, and not just because of the piano. But could I really? I don't even know this boy. Does he really mean it, or is he just being polite?

I absently pull one of my braids in front of me and play with the end, a nervous habit my mom likes to correct me about. "I don't want to intrude."

"Nah, it'd be cool."

I smile tentatively.

"It'd be nice," he adds.

I grin. "Well, okay. Maybe."

He smiles and my heart really lets loose this time. He's cute and sweet and can play the piano like the devil. Oh yeah. I could crush on this boy hard.

"Good." He's still smiling. I turn to let myself through the gate. Rather than closing it between us, he steps out onto the green. "Tomorrow?"

I smile. I hesitate. Finally I say, "Okay."

"Cool. See you tomorrow, Ashley."

My heart hasn't slowed one bit. "Okay. Bye, Erik."

We give each other shy waves goodbye and I head back toward the Greenbelt. Halfway there I look back. He's gone, but still, I wait until I'm back on the path and truly out of sight before I give a little skip and clasp my hands to my chest. I can't wait for tomorrow.

Chapter 3

Friday of that week, Erik and I are sitting cross-legged on the floor of his living room, sheet music from the bookcase in haphazard stacks around us. I did go back on Tuesday, and have been back every day this week. I already feel like we've been friends for months instead of only a few days.

I still haven't met his parents, since I have to be home well before they tend to walk in the door. His dad is a high-end lawyer and his mom is the CFO of a cosmetics company with locations in five different states. Erik told me half the time they're not even home for dinner.

I did finally tell my parents about my new friend, mainly so I could stay longer without arousing suspicion, but I didn't mention that we're here alone. Even though Erik and I haven't so much as kissed, my dad would go ballistic if he knew I was alone with a boy like this. (That's the reason my mom and I decided not to tell my dad when Bernie Shepherd kissed me after Prom last year. Bernie and I never really turned into much, so there was no reason to freak my dad out about nothing.)

Besides, me being here is kinda sorta innocent, if you don't count the way Erik makes my heart flutter when I'm with him or the fantasizing I do about him when I'm not.

Every day I've returned, he's already been changed out of his school uniform. Today, he's wearing jeans and a plain, black tee that makes him look extra hot. I'm wearing my favorite stonewashed jeans and a flowy peasant top. "This is a good one." Erik holds up the little booklet of sheet music so I can see the title.

It's a classical piece by Chopin, but I'm not familiar with it. I take it from him and open it up so I can look over the measures. As I go, I can hear it in my head. Actually, I think I might have heard this one before but I'm not sure. I hum a few bars. "Like that?"

He nods. "Have you played it?"

"Nope." I close the book and add it to the "Songs to Learn" pile. I've already played him many of the songs I know, and he's played me several of his as well. We're looking through his stash of music to see what I should learn to play next. I've noticed some of the songs have hand-written notations at various places along the measures.

"I don't know how I'm going to pick just one." I pull another book off the shelf.

"Maybe you should stop looking for more then," he teases. "Besides, these aren't going anywhere, you know."

"I guess." I continue flipping through the book. "Hey, I know this one!"

"I haven't learned that one yet." He scoots closer to me and looks over my shoulder. My heart rate increases in response, but I'm pretty good at holding it together around him. I even survived watching an episode of Lost on his fancy, new iPad yesterday, and that was with his shoulder pressed against mine almost the entire time. I didn't fall in love with the series as much as he promised me I would, but I still agreed to watch the rest with him some time. Because, you know, the shoulder.

"It's a fun song." I tap the page with my finger. "You should play it while I finally pick something. Then it'll be my turn."

I plop the book in his lap and scoot the "Songs to Learn" pile closer to me.

"I told you, silly, I don't know this song."

I look at him and furrow my brows. "Can't you read music?"

He laughs. "Uh, <u>yeah</u> I can read music. But you can't just sit down and start playing a song you don't know."

"Well, it doesn't have to be <u>perfect.</u>" I smile wickedly. It's only been four days and I already know a way to tease him.

He rolls his eyes and stands up, holding the music. "I'm not a perfectionist."

"Are too." I start spreading the stack in front of me, hoping there will be one clear winner among them, but so far there isn't. Ugh, how will I ever choose? I want to play all of them right now.

Erik has settled himself on the bench behind me and begins to play. As usual, listening to him causes me to stop what I'm doing. But this time, it's for a different reason. He keeps stumbling at various places, and once even goes back and redoes a measure before going forward in the piece again.

I'm surprised how much he's fumbling through it. When he gets to the end, he nods. "Yeah, that's cool. Maybe I'll learn this one next."

He turns and smiles down at me. I'm not sure what to say. What I'm thinking is, <u>Don't you know how to read music better than that?</u>

My phone dings and I pull it out of my pocket to check it.

Mom: Remember we have to leave at five sharp.

"Oh right." I check the time. "Dang it. I have to go."

I text back a quick: <u>K.</u>

"Right." He sounds a little disappointed. "Movie night."

I nod. Movie Night has been a Morrison family tradition for a couple years now. Usually we just rent something from

Redbox, but every now and then we splurge and go to the dollar theatre, like tonight.

"I've still never heard of a family that uses up their senior daughter's Friday night every single week." Now it's his turn to tease me.

"I think that's the point. That way I can't get into trouble with boys."

Erik gives me a grin that makes my cheeks hot. I smile and look away, gathering the music back into a pile again. "Should we put this back on the shelves?"

"Did you pick a song?"

"I can't. There's too many good ones. Will you pick one for me?"

"Okay. You can leave it. I'll put it away. I know you have to go."

I sigh and stand. As he walks me to the back gate, like he always does, I realize I'm not sure how weekends fit into our friendship. I've been coming every day after school, but what happens tomorrow? Then I have to remind myself that he probably doesn't want to see me every day. I mean, we just met. And probably he does stuff with his family on the weekends. Or, maybe he does. Actually, I'm not so sure.

"So..." he says hesitantly, after we go through the gate.

"So..." I say hesitantly too, "um... shall I come work on it... next week sometime?"

He looks at me, holding my gaze. Those beautiful, deep brown eyes. Oh man, my heart's really going now. I wonder, not for the first time, what it would be like to kiss Erik Williams.

"What are you doing tomorrow?"

I smile and shrug. "Nothing much. Chores in the morning, but nothing after that."

He smiles, too. "Nothing in the afternoon?"

I shake my head. The way he's smiling at me makes me feel bold. "Want to play then?" I suggest.

His smile falters a bit before he hitches it back on. "I was thinking we could go for a walk on the Greenbelt. I feel guilty I've been keeping you from your walks."

"Oh, okay. That'd be cool." I actually really like the idea of a walk with Erik, but something about the way he responded to my suggestion is nagging me, way in the back of my head.

"Want to meet at the sign?" He gestures to the "Private" sign next to the Greenbelt. "Say, one o'clock?"

"Sure," I say smiling. "See you then."

I hurry back home, but that nagging feeling follows me the whole way.

When I get to the sign five minutes to one the next day, Erik is already there waiting for me. He's wearing shorts and a sleeveless athletic top and when I see him I think I'm going to die. His arms are long and sinewy and defined. His legs are tanned and muscular. I remember now something he told me on Tuesday—that he likes to go for runs on the Greenbelt—but I forgot. I guess we've both neglected our love for the Greenbelt this past week.

He smiles and slowly starts toward me when he sees me. I think I see his eyes sweep up and down my body—I'm in my plaid shorts and a snug tee—but I'm not sure.

"Hey," he says, as I draw near.

"Hey. Which way do you want to go?"

"Whatever you want."

"Let's go that way." I point farther down the Greenbelt. I miss my bridge and like the idea of going there with him.

He agrees and we head down the path. Almost immediately, an awkward silence swells between us. I'm not sure what to say. It occurs to me that maybe we don't really have much in common outside of the piano. But at the same time, I know that's not really true because we've talked about plenty of other things. Why does it feel so awkward right now?

"How was the movie last night?" he asks.

Relieved to have something to say, I start telling him about it. And just like that, the awkward part is over and we're chatting easily. When we get to the bridge, we don't stop at the top like I usually do. We continue on, entertaining each other with funny stories about our teachers. His chemistry teacher last year sounds like a crazy old coot and I think my chemistry class would have been a helluva lot more interesting if I'd had someone as entertaining as that guy.

I'm pleased to see that whenever there's a little hidden footpath that breaks away toward the river, Erik likes to follow them as much as I do. Even though I've already been down them all, I love winding through the trees, ducking under branches, and going right up to the river's edge where the water plays its music best.

When we head down these little paths, it feels more intimate, too. Like we're all alone in the world. It's even more private than when we're in his home all by ourselves, but I'm not sure why. Still, every time we go back to the main Greenbelt with its broad, tree-lined lane and occasional jogger, I'm disappointed to leave the privacy behind.

Our conversation has lingered on school and I've taken to asking him questions about the private school he attends. In some ways it sounds different than what I know—his school is definitely smaller—but in other ways it's the same: classes, teachers, homework. He makes it sound less like a foreign world and more like what I guess it is: just a school.

We get to the point on the Greenbelt where I usually turn around and go back, but we keep going. I like that I'm discovering something new with him.

There are new side paths to follow, some as faint as a deer trail. One leads to an inviting grassy area shaded by a massive oak.

"This is nice," he says. "Wanna sit here?"

"Sure." I find a soft spot and sit down. He sits down next to me, but lays all the way back, tucking his hands behind his head. I grin and lay down next to him, pulling my braids in front and resting my hands on my stomach. My shoulder is touching his arm and feeling all electric about it.

The broad canopy of branches arches above us. Their dark arms spider out against the bright green of the leaves, blue sky peeking through.

"This is the best way to look at a tree," I say.

"Yeah."

My attention's a little divided though. I really want to kiss him. But I've only known him a week and maybe he only wants to be friends. I don't want to mess anything up. Besides, I've only ever let one guy kiss me. I've never been the one to make the first move. So I'm just going to lay here feeling tingly and play with the end of my braid and pretend I'm very, very interested in looking at the tree.

He rolls toward me slightly and my heart catches in my throat. He was just retrieving his phone out of his pocket.

"Are you game for episode two of <u>Lost</u>?"

"Here?" I'm still not used to the idea of watching movies on phones and tablets. The Morrison house isn't exactly down with the latest technology. "Wouldn't it be more comfortable at your place?"

His smile falters and he hesitates.

Now I know what the nagging feeling was from yesterday. "You don't want me to meet your parents," I say, a sick feeling settling in the pit my stomach. "Do you?"

He puts his phone on his stomach and looks back up at the branches. "No," he says simply.

"Because I'm not rich?" I didn't mean to say it, but I do think it.

He looks at me quickly. "What? Of course not. Do you think I care about that?"

I shrug. "I don't know."

"So are you my friend only because I have money?"

"No!"

"Well, how is it different?"

I exhale. "Okay, maybe it's not. But why don't you want me to meet your parents?"

He faces back to the tree again, and says with a dull voice, "It's my dad, mostly. He's just kind of... hard to get used to."

I frown. "What do you mean?"

"Well, he's just hard in general. I don't know. I don't want to make you uncomfortable. And I guess I don't want to be uncomfortable."

Wow. Is his dad really that bad?

"I'm sorry," he says.

He's frowning and starting to look a little upset. I lightly bump his arm with mine. "Hey. It's okay."

He looks at me and I give him a smile.

He's still frowning. "It's really not you. I think you're great."

My smile broadens and I feel the heat rising to my cheeks. I hate it when I blush! I bump him with my arm again. "Are we going to watch <u>Lost</u> or what?"

So we do. By the end of episode two, I'm hooked and ask for more. Somehow my head has ended up resting on his arm. I don't mind that either. We binge watch four more episodes and only stop because we're both starving and his battery's nearly dead.

"Next time we need to bring snacks," he says on our way back down the Greenbelt.

"Definitely." I'm pleased that he's already talking about a next time.

When we get to the bridge, I slow my steps so it's easier to stop at the top. He follows my lead and we lean on the rail, looking at the river stretching away from us. His arm is pressed against mine, shoulder to elbow. Still looking at the water, he bumps me gently with his hip. I smile and bump him back.

We look at each other, both grinning. Our eyes lock in a way they haven't before.

My heart is pounding more than it ever has around him, because I think he's going to kiss me. I hold his eyes because I want him to. Then just like that, like it's the easiest thing in the world, Erik Williams leans in and gives me a kiss. His lips are so soft on mine, I think I'm going to float away over the river. This is nothing like the awkward kiss Bernie Shepherd gave me.

Erik pulls away slowly. We both smile at each other and I look down at the river, blushing. I feel silly, like a little kid, but also amazing, like something big inside me is different now. Still smiling, I glance at him. His eyes are still on me and he's giving me a look that makes me feel weak. I want to kiss him again, but I'm not sure how to manage it. Still smiling, I hold his eyes and lean in the tiniest bit. It turns out that's all it takes.

His lips press against mine again. I love him this close to me. This time his fingertips just barely brush the underside of my jaw. I think my knees are going to give out. Part of me wants to keep going, but the other part of me feels a little relieved when he pulls away. I think this is all I can handle for the moment.

This is definitely nothing like kissing Bernie. By comparison, Bernie and I were kids playing at something. But with Erik, everything feels more real.

"Come on." He gently nudges me with his shoulder. He pulls my hand into his and we take our time going back.

Chapter 4

I didn't get to see him Sunday—his family actually had plans—but we've finally exchanged numbers, so we've texted plenty. I offered some speculation on the future of Sun and Jin in <u>Lost</u>, but he wouldn't say if I was right or not. We also discussed which song he should teach me first and finally settled on a sonata by Clementi. After a brief kiss when I showed up at his house today after school, we got straight to it. He already had the sheet music on the piano, waiting for me.

"This is different from the one I saw," I say as we settle next to each other on the bench.

"I got you a copy so you could make your own notes on it."

I roll my eyes. "Well that defeats the whole purpose of borrowing what you have here."

He shrugs. "Go ahead and run through it, then we can talk about it."

He's taking on what I imagine to be the demeanor of a piano teacher starting a lesson. It's adorable. Also, pretty exciting. I want to learn whatever he's willing to teach me.

I turn my attention to the sheet music and do what I usually do before starting on a brand new piece. I keep my hands on my lap and run my eyes along the music. I keep proper time, hearing the music in my head as I go along, and imagine my fingers playing the chords. When I get to the end, I take a deep breath, place my fingers on the keys (I'm still so in love with this piano), and play what I just heard in my head.

It always sounds so much better in real life. Imagining it in my mind is one thing, but when the music is really here it's like it's been set free and wants to climb to the rafters. And these rafters are a lot higher than the music room at school! I'm still not done drooling over how much better the acoustics are in this house.

Even though I'm deep in the rabbit hole of the music, as I run over the places I know I could play better with practice, or differently now that I've tried it once and think I know a better way, I mentally make note of them like I always do. I'll ask Erik about those places first. I'm not as polished as he is, I can hear that clearly. I want to try to learn what he knows.

When I finish the song and emerge back in the real world, I can't help clasping my hands to my chest. "Good choice! I love the little flourishes in the middle. Right here." I put my finger to the place and smile. I'm still all tingly from the music.

I turn to him, grinning, but he's scrutinizing me with a serious expression.

Uh oh. "Was it that bad?"

He doesn't answer me. His expression doesn't change at all. "Are you messing with me?"

"Huh?"

He doesn't answer. Instead he gets off the bench and goes to the bookcase behind us.

After only a moment's consideration, he pulls a book off the shelf and opens it up, flipping the pages sharply. I want to ask him what's wrong, but I'm afraid to know. Instead I watch him and fidget with the end of my braid and try not to flinch when he sits down and puts the open book in front of me.

"Ever play this?" He gestures at it impatiently.

I read the title. I don't recognize the piece but I don't answer right away. Instead I go over several measures to make sure I don't know the tune. "No."

Something's wrong, but I don't know what.

"Go ahead then." He doesn't sound angry. More like... determined.

For a brief moment I consider saying no. I don't know what's going on. I don't know that I want to play. If he's picking my playing apart, well then why doesn't he help me? I can hear the difference in our playing, but how am I supposed to know how to make it better without help? It's been a long time since I've had anyone around to tell me what I need to fix. It's not like that's my fault.

But I focus on the sheet music in front of me anyway. I go over it mentally first, starting back at the beginning. The whole time, I sense him watching me. Why is he watching me like that?

When I finish my reading I almost say I won't play until he tells me what's wrong, but the song I just read is lilting around in my head and my fingers are itching to bring it to life.

It occurs to me this may be the last time I ever play his piano. That's what gets me moving more than anything. I want to hear this song on this piano. I may not be trained like he is, but I know enough to know the piano at school won't do this song justice.

So I play. And before I fall into the hole the music always creates, I think, screw him, because if he's not going to help me or if he's going to send me home, then I'm going to play it how I like it. Eyes glued to the sheet music, I follow along and bid my fingers to do their part. The song swells inside me. I run through a set of measures so goddamned amazing to play, I'd stop and play them again just for fun if I were alone, but I keep going.

It's over too quickly, and when it is, I've never in my life felt more vulnerable in front of another person as I do now. Because I know it's not how it would sound if he were the one playing it. Besides that, I'm not going to play any more songs until he tells me what's wrong, and maybe once he tells me what's wrong I still won't want to play.

I turn to him, matching his frown with one of my own. "Okay, what?" I demand.

He blinks at me.

I exhale forcefully. "You're kind of freaking me out. Would you just spit it out already?"

"You really never played that before." He says it like a statement, not a question.

I answer anyway. "No. Obviously."

"You <u>swear?</u> You're not messing around with me?"

"Erik, will you please tell me what's wrong?"

He breaks out into a smile. Then he starts laughing a little. Then he starts laughing a lot.

59

"What?" I'm still irritated and more confused than ever.

"You're a freaking prodigy or something and you're, like, completely clueless about it."

I can't say why, but I feel slapped. My face is getting hot and not because he's cute. He continues to laugh, but I'm scowling. "Stop," I say quietly.

"How are you even doing that?" he says, apparently not hearing me. "That was fucking amazing."

I'm not an idiot. I know my playing isn't up to snuff. I don't play like he can. So why is he acting like this? "Cut it out." I hop off the bench and pace away from him, folding my arms. I'm rewarded with the view of the green and the pond, but I'm too angry to enjoy it. He's the one messing with me, and it's not funny.

"Hey," he says softer now, just a trace of lingering laughter on his voice. "What's wrong?"

"What's wrong?" I spin, arms still crossed. His smile disappears as he takes in my fuming expression. "What the hell was all that?" I gesture to the music.

He blinks in surprise. I thought he was playing a game with me, but now that I see the confusion on his face, I'm not so sure. I don't know what's going on. We stare at one another a moment. Some of the hardness between us slowly softens, but I'm still guarded. I still don't know what just happened.

"Hey." He raises his hands in surrender and slowly slides off the bench toward me. "Sorry. I didn't mean to make you mad."

"I'm not mad." But my arms are still crossed. I know I'm lying.

He stops half way between me and the piano. "I'm sorry I..." he says softly, then stops. "Maybe you don't know this, but you're pretty amazing in the sight reading department."

I'm still frowning, but my arms slowly unfold and come to my side.

"I thought you were tricking me or something," he continues. "Most people can't read like that. There are a few pianists in the professional world who are known for being able to sit down and sight-read well enough to be concert ready, but most of us have to actually practice. We have to get familiar with it to play it well all the way through."

I shrug. I still don't think I get it. "Aren't you supposed to be able to read music?" God, the hours I spent training my fingers to follow along. Was that stupid? Is that not how people do it?

"Sure. You're just crazy good at it."

I still feel kind of weird. I wish this hadn't happened. I'm not even sure why.

He puts one hand on my shoulder. "Hey, it's a good thing. Okay?"

It's not until this moment that I realize that what I thought was anger inside of me, was really fear. My mom says there's usually a softer emotion hiding under anger's fierceness, but I don't want to talk about any of this anymore.

"Look... can we just... play? I thought you were going to teach me some stuff."

"Yeah." He squeezes my shoulder and drops his hand. "I can teach you some things."

"Okay." I'm trying to let my earlier panic slide away. "That's better. Cuz you said you would."

He smiles at me and I give him a half smile back.

"I will. Come on."

We get to work and it doesn't take long for the tension of our argument, or whatever it was, to slide away. Soon, we're back to having fun. Even though I don't have anything to compare it to, I think he's a good teacher.

After a couple times through the song, he takes a chance and leans over to kiss me. I willingly kiss him back. We lose our focus a bit after that, and have difficulty making it all the way through a song without kissing each other. Finally we give up altogether and end up moving our practice session to the couch.

A few weeks later, it's Movie Night again. Tonight's pick is from our own collection—Freedom Writers—and this time, Erik's joined us. He's been to my house for dinner a couple of times, but this is the first time he came for the movie. I'm amazed at how easily he's fit in with my family. My mom loves him and he gets along well with my dad. It doesn't hurt that Erik has sense enough to keep a respectable distance between us when we're with my parents. My dad keeps an eagle eye on us anyway. Only my mom knows Erik and I have kissed, but even she thinks there's been nothing more than a peck goodbye at the end of our dates. Or maybe she's feigning ignorance for my sake, because part of me thinks she has to know better.

I still haven't met Erik's parents. Given what he's told me about them, I'm not in much of a hurry. They sound kind of intense.

Erik and I are sitting next to each other on the couch, not touching, and my dad is on the other side of me. He's wearing his beat up jeans and petting the cat, Missy, who's crawled up onto his chest. Missy is technically mine, but she really only likes my dad. She follows him around and gets under his feet until he's tripping over her gray, furry body and cursing that we should've bought a dog. But the fact that he lets her lay all over him betrays his true feelings.

My mom is sitting cross-legged on the floor in front of my dad, her flowing skirt in a puddle around her. She's wearing a bold-patterned top, her long, straight hair hangs past her shoulders, and she has no makeup on other than some lip stick. When Erik first met her, he said she looked like a hippie, which sounds about right. My mother was named after Susan B. Anthony. When I was a child and first learned about such a thing as feminism and women's rights, I couldn't quite wrap my brain around it. It had never occurred to me that I might be denied something simply for being a girl. I think my mom is the reason why. She's quietly larger than life, my mom.

As the credits roll, we slowly start to shift in our seats and stretch our legs. "Ah," Mom says, getting to her feet and going to our old combo DVD/VCR player. "Such a good film. And an important one." Freedom Writers is a true story about a teacher finding a way to reach students at a tough high school in LA. "What do you think would happen if all students in situations like that were given hope and a voice?"

"There'd be a lot less violence," I say. Too often, violence is borne of the desperation and hopelessness consuming otherwise decent people. I wonder, not for the first time, what I would be like if I were raised in the darkest pockets of the inner city like the kids in the movie. Who would I be? It makes me grateful for what I have, such as it is. I wonder what Erik thinks about it. He's even further removed from the inner city than I am.

I glance at him. He's quiet, and has a thoughtful look on his face. This is different fare from our usual Lost, that's for sure.

"What do you think, Erik?" my mom prompts. Erik's mentioned that he's not used to being asked so many questions. He's told me my parents are kind of like the teachers at school, except nicer. I get the impression his parents don't ask him what he thinks much, but that's just always the way it's been in my house.

"It's sad," Erik says simply. "And frustrating."

"Why is it frustrating?" my dad asks easily.

"Because there's no fixing that." Erik gestures toward the TV, which my mom just turned off. "I mean, yeah one teacher can help one class, but what about everyone else at that school? What about all the other schools like it?"

My mom nods. "There will always be imbalance and unfairness in the world, that's true. But there will also always be people who do what they can to make the world a good place to be. We just have to decide which side of the fight we want to be on."

Erik furrows his brows. "It makes me feel kind of guilty."

"You can't help that your parents are wealthy," my dad says. "You're just a kid. You don't need to feel guilty."

Erik looks at him suddenly, clearly taken aback. Frankly, I am too. Even my mom gives dad a look. My dad has never brought up Erik's wealth before now. He's never ranted about the neighborhood Erik lives in.

He's never said the slightest thing about it to embarrass me, but now here's this. I wonder if my dad's disdain for the wealthy came through in his tone, or if I was only able to pick up on it because I know him so well.

"I wasn't talking about that," Erik says, still looking at my dad like something new has been revealed and he's still taking it in. "I was talking about the fact that—" and here his eyes swing to my mother, maybe because he senses she will be his ally, "—what I'm going to do with my life is pretty selfish. I'm going to be a pianist. How is that helping the world?"

She gives him a broad smile. "Of course that's helping the world! We need music and art and stories. It's part of what makes the world a beautiful place. We need people to make those things for us, like you and Ashley do."

She says this in that easy way of hers, and I'm grateful for the way she's keeping things light.

"Now you kids get going. Your dad and I need some snuggle time."

"Mom," I say, rolling my eyes and getting up.

"Back by eleven-thirty," my dad says firmly, as Erik gets off the couch too.

"Want us to bring you back anything?" I ask. Erik and I are headed to Sonic for ice cream.

My parents both shake their heads as my mom sits next to my dad, who puts his arm around her shoulders. For as long as I can remember, the hours past nine belong to my parents. It used to be I'd head to my room to do my own thing, but Erik is starting to become part of the routine.

We say our goodbyes, and as soon as we're out the front door, Erik slides his arm around my waist. I wrap my arm around him too. I've been missing his touch all night. We get to his car—a brand-new Subaru Legacy his parents gave him for his sixteenth birthday—but before we get in, we embrace each other and slide into a deep kiss. I must say, I've gotten pretty good at this kind of kissing and there's no question Erik knows what to do with his lips and his tongue.

My whole body is humming and I want more, but we keep it short in case my father decides to peek out the window. Erik opens my door for me and I climb in, relieved to be alone with him at last.

As he gets in and starts the car, I kick off my sandals and tuck my feet under me. "Sorry about my dad."

Erik shrugs. "It's fine."

I don't know if it really is fine, but I don't press it. My dad rants about the rich, but I think with Erik it's more personal than that. He knows the neighborhood Erik lives in and our house just isn't much in comparison. There's no getting around it.

"I like your parents," Erik says, not for the first time. "And I like being at your house. It's comfortable."

I smile. "My mom likes you. She says you're sweet."

He smiles. "My devious plan is working."

I laugh. "My dad likes you too, you know."

Erik nods, but doesn't say anything. Instead he reaches over and takes my hand, driving with one hand on top of the steering wheel.

"I like how your mom talks about music." He turns onto the main road.

"What do you mean?"

"Well, for her it's about giving something beautiful to the world."

"Well, it is, right? Isn't that how you see it, too?"

He nods. "But my parents are different. With them, it's more..."

He hesitates. There's something else brewing underneath. I want to know what it is. "What?"

"It's more about what I'm supposed to get out of it, or what they can get out of it. You know, the prestige and all that."

He's told me before about how hard his parents push him. It started when he showed promise at a very young age. His first piano teacher recognized it and referred him to Boise's premier tutor, Mr. Lamont. Even being able to work with him was an accomplishment. Ever since then, Erik's parents have taken a keen interest in things.

"But music isn't about that for you, right? You're not in it for the prestige."

He shrugs. "I don't know. I've... kind of always had it, so how would I know? Maybe that's what I want, too."

"Pshhh," I say and he grins at me. "I've seen you play, remember? You can't fake that kind of passion."

He gives me a playful smile. "Gotcha fooled, huh?"

I lightly smack his shoulder and lean my head back against the seat, smiling at him.

He glances at me and gives me a wicked grin. Damn, he's so good-looking. I smile more broadly and look at our intertwined hands. I take my other hand and run my fingertips along his fingers. He squeezes me in response.

When he pulls into Sonic, he chooses a stall farthest from the building. My heart beats thickly, hoping he parked here for the same reason I would have if I were the one driving. We talk about music and order our treats—a sundae for him and a small chocolate shake for me—and continue to chat and laugh until the car hop brings us our order.

A few bites in, he drops his spoon in his little plastic bowl. He leans over, cups his hand around the back of my neck, and pulls me in for the kind of kiss my dad would flip over if he saw it.

He caught me off guard, but I recover from the surprise quickly, kissing him back. Our tongues are cool and sweet from the ice cream, but warm up quickly. Even though we're both holding our ice cream, we continue to kiss. Erik tastes like heaven. Kissing him is like playing music: the world disappears and it's only him and me, the soft sounds of our breathing enveloping us.

Slowly, I set down my cup, still kissing him. He follows my lead. Ice cream abandoned, he rubs his hand down my back and over my hip, leaving a trail of electricity in his wake. Right there in the far reaches of the Sonic parking lot. I never would have imagined such a thing a month ago. But Erik is changing my life. He's changing me. And I only want more.

Chapter 5

A month later, I'm curled up on Erik's couch, my school bag and Keds on the floor next to me. I'm watching him practice his piece for an upcoming recital. It's a private recital his teacher puts on twice a year for his students and their families. Erik offered to ask his teacher if I could participate, but I wasn't interested. I'm not paying for lessons; I shouldn't be there. Erik's still trying to get me to participate in something called Music Fest, though. It's a twice-yearly competition for local, young pianists. Anyone can get in, so long as they pay the $25 entry fee.

"My teacher says it's important to perform as much as possible," Erik had told me. "It's good experience."

But I can't bring myself to agree. As I sit here listening to him, I'm overwhelmed as I always am by the power of his playing. I just don't know if I can get up on the same stage he does and pretend to think I belong there.

I watch his face and his hands as he plays. He's so passionate about it. It's one of the things I love about him. I may not be able to play like him, but love for the music itself is definitely something we share.

When he finishes I give a satisfied sigh. "I wish I could play like that," I say smiling. I absently pull one of my braids around to the front and pull off the tie at the end. I tend to reset my braids once or twice a day. Mom thinks it's a nervous habit, but I think it's because there's something soothing about running a brush through my hair. "You're so good, Erik."

He slides off the bench. "You're just saying that because you like the way I kiss."

I grin as I start running my fingers through the braid to undo it, working from the bottom up. "You'll never know."

"How's the run in the middle sounding?" he asks seriously. "Better?"

I nod. "You've got it."

"Mr. Lamont thinks I should use it for my Festival piece."

"I thought you wanted to play the Mozart one." That's the piece I've been working on the last week or so and I'm in love with it. Erik's mentioned wanting to learn that one next.

"I was thinking you could play the Mozart piece for Music Fest."

I sigh. I've finished undoing the first braid and pull around the second one. "Erik—"

"Just hear me out." He gently takes my braid out of my hand and slowly pulls out the tie. I sigh again and sit forward on the couch a bit, giving him room to work. He's loves playing with my hair—and I love him doing it—so I get the sense he's trying to soften me up.

"You're working it up into this big thing." He's running his fingers through the braid and making me go all mushy inside. He's totally not playing fair. "But it's not as scary as it sounds. The competition part really isn't that big a deal. Really. Most kids at Music Fest don't place. It's more about getting experience playing in front of an audience."

Oh my gosh, even the word audience makes me all jittery. "I don't know." I reach into my bag, retrieve my brush, and hand it to him just as he finishes undoing the braid. He runs his fingers through my hair first, then takes the brush and starts running it over my scalp and down through my hair. I close my eyes. It feels twice as good when he does it.

"Come on. It'll be good for you. It'll help you not be so afraid."

"I'm not afraid."

He laughs softly and leans in to whisper in my ear, "Liar." The sound of his voice tingles through my body.

He returns to brushing my hair and I look back at him. He's smiling at me. I turn away. "Okay, fine. I'm scared. I don't have the experience you have though."

"Well, this is how you can change that."

"Stop pushing me," I say in a teasing voice.

"You need someone pushing you." He's being light too, but I hear the seriousness underneath. His parents push him, so that's all he knows, but I find that hard to relate to. No one pushed me to watch all those YouTube videos or spend hours of my free time practicing at school. I did that on my own.

I think Erik has his own wings, too, and would probably be exactly where he is now whether his parents pushed him or not. So part of me wants to resist him.

Yet.

Whether I've pushed myself or not, here I am afraid to step foot on a stage.

"You gotta start somewhere, Ashley."

I sigh. "I don't know."

"Well..." he runs the brush through my hair again, root all the way to the tip. "Think about it. Okay?"

I don't answer. I don't want to think about it. But I am.

He continues to slowly brush out my hair. Neither one of us speak. He's making me want to make out with him, but I wait, enjoying the anticipation. I never knew brushing hair could be so sexy until Erik first did it. By the time he places the brush on the floor, my heart's pounding and my breathing is shallow.

I turn to face him and he pulls me into the crook of his arm, a sexy look on his face.

He leans backwards and brings me with him, out of sight of the windows.

On top of him now, I look at him as my hair falls down around us on either side. We're in our own little world again. We hold each other's gaze. He brushes the back of his fingers along my jawline, then gently hooks a finger under my chin and brings my lips down to his.

It's a sweet kiss at first. Not the tentative kind that marked the start of our relationship. It's the kind of sweet kiss that seems to say something.

For the first time, it occurs to me that I might be falling in love with Erik Williams. But how would I know? I've never been in love before.

He parts his lips slightly and I part mine, too. The tips of our tongues touch and it's electric. His hands on my back increase their pressure. I press into him too, with my whole body. We slide into a deeper kiss then, our eagerness for each other rising. His hands begin to wander, running under my thick hair. One hand dips down and curves around my rear end.

My hands are wandering too. I slip one under his shirt, the heat in my body rising as I run my fingers along his firm abdomen and up to his chest. He slides his hand under my shirt too. His touch leaves pulses of pleasure on my bare skin.

Our tongues taste and swirl around each other with more intensity. He fumbles with the hook on my bra for a moment, then I feel the release that indicates success.

His arms tighten around me and we break our kiss as he rolls us over so he's on top of me. I feel his erection on my upper thigh. He brushes back the loose strands of my hair to expose my neck and drops his lips to it.

I exhale a shaky breath as he starts sucking on the sensitive skin on my neck. God, this is almost my favorite thing. His hand runs up my bare stomach, slides under my bra, and caresses me. This is my favorite thing.

It's funny how quickly we get to this place these days.

I hold him tighter and dip my mouth down so I can taste his neck. He arches his head back, exhaling. I always get so heady when I know I'm giving him pleasure, too. I increase my attentions on the crook of his neck, where I know he likes it best, and get him to moan.

His caresses send shivers all over my body, yet I'm hot everywhere. I pull up his shirt to expose more of his skin and our bare stomachs press against each other.

He rearranges his hips slightly and angles into me. His hardness presses against the tendon between my leg and my sex. I'm taken aback a bit, because he's never done that before. When he does it again, I surprise myself by angling my hips to match his pressure against me.

With that, we kick into a new gear. He returns to my mouth and we kiss each other eagerly. He pulls my shirt up further until my bra is exposed. Then he pulls up my bra. I'm panting and dizzy with the heat of what we're doing to each other. I bend one knee and hook my ankle around his leg. We grind our pelvises together and now I'm the one moaning.

I'm starting to feel carried away into an area I'm not sure I'm ready for. But as he kisses my neck and slowly starts working his way down, I don't want to stop him either. In fact, I really, really want him to keep going.

I rub my hands along his firm shoulders, my eyes closed and my head arched back. He slowly works his way down, maybe proceeding with caution. I could tell him to stop, but I don't. He keeps going and my breath hitches in my chest. He's so close. Closer, and I open my eyes to look down at him. I'm fully exposed and his eyes are closed as he kisses my skin. He stops just before he gets to my nipple. Maybe he's not sure if I'm okay with this. I raise my chest slightly. I want it.

He takes me into his mouth and my head falls back, my eyes closed. I'm tingling more than I ever thought possible. He sucks on me again and again and I wonder how he knows what to do down there. The other one starts to ache with wanting.

That feeling that maybe we're going too far increases a bit, but so does my wanting more of his touch. He runs his tongue around my nipple and I think I'm going to die, it feels so good. He breaks away and kisses the valley on my chest once, twice, before going to the other side. I gasp and grab the hair on the back of his head.

We kick into yet another gear. Part of me needs to stop, but the other part of me needs to keep going. Our hands aren't caressing anymore, they're groping. He sucks on me a bit longer then comes back up to kiss me and our mouths meet with a different kind of urgency than we ever have before. We're kissing so deeply and panting and rubbing our hands all over each other. His erection is right over my tender place and I've wrapped both of my legs around his thighs. I don't remember bringing them up. Now I really do feel swept away by something that's too much. It's way too much.

I lower my legs and break our kiss. "Okay," I say panting. I kiss him again, mouth closed. I'm still fighting the urges in my own body, but I'm decided. "Okay," I say again.

He lifts off me slightly and readjusts so his hardness isn't pressing on me anymore. "Sorry," he breathes. He's panting too.

"No, it's okay." I kiss him again. "I just... I need to stop." I give him a smile that's half embarrassment, half I really liked that.

He grins back and lifts off me more. We shuffle around as he pulls his shirt down, and I get my bra back in place and pull my shirt down with my bra still unhooked. I'll have to sit up to set that right again, but I'm not ready to get up just yet.

I give him another kiss. It's open, but gentler than what we were just doing. It feels more like a conclusion than a restart. He settles his weight on me again and kisses me back. When we finish he pulls away and scoots so he's more to the side of me, only partially laying on me. One of his legs is slightly bent over mine. He props his head on his hand and smiles down at me. I wonder again if I'm in love with him. What does being in love feel like? Does it feel like this? Because this feels pretty incredible.

I smile at him. "I really like you."

He grins and gives a little laugh. "I really like you too," as if that was the most obvious thing in the world. I pull up and give him an enthusiastic kiss.

We started playful, but before I know it our kissing is heating up again. Grinning, I pull away and push lightly on his chest. "No, no, no. Let's don't start that again."

"Are you sure?" he says with a wink, but he crawls off me and grabs both my hands to pull me into a sit.

We both take a deep breath then kind of laugh and grin at each other, as if to say, "Well <u>that</u> was an experience." I reach back under my shirt to tend to my bra, and am glad when he looks away to give me my privacy.

"Your turn to play," he says, meaning the piano.

"You go. I need to do my hair."

At the same time he's getting up, he smooths back a section of my hair and gives me a peck. "We mussed you up a bit," he says grinning. He heads to the piano, and I gather up my ties and brush and head to the bathroom. When I see my reflection, my eyebrows raise because my hair really is embarrassingly messy. That teaches us to make out that heavy with my hair down, I guess.

I run a brush through it and rapidly work my long tresses into a double braid. I hardly have to think about it, I've had so much practice. When I come out of the bathroom, he's at the piano but still hasn't started playing.

"What have you been doing?"

"Just getting your music ready. Come on. It's your turn."

I sit down and see he's set up the piece he wants me to play at Music Fest. I purse my lips but say nothing. Instead I play. For the first time, the fact that he's sitting next to me flows into my awareness of the music and becomes part of it. It's the song and it's Erik and it's us and it's amazing.

I think I'm in love.

My hands fly over the keys and I smile. His hand rests lightly on my back.

"What's this?"

The voice that booms across the living room is so deep and loud and carries so well it brings everything to a halt. My hands flinch off the keys and I look up to see Erik's dad standing in the entryway to the living room, frowning at us.

Erik's hand leaves my back and he puts his hands on his lap.

"Hi, Dad," he says calmly. Like, crazy calm. I feel like I've been caught doing something horrible and cringe to think what would've happened if his dad had walked in ten minutes ago. My mind fumbles around, trying to get a grasp on things. I vaguely wonder if it's past dinner time or something, but it's still light out. It's maybe only five o'clock. I've been seeing Erik for almost two months now and his dad has never been home this early.

"This is my friend, Ashley," Erik says in the same calm voice.

I smile and offer a weak, "Hello."

Erik's dad is still frowning at us.

"She's a piano student too. We're just practicing."

His dad offers a stiff, formal "Hello" that has 'prosecuting attorney' written all over it. He's not frowning any more but he isn't exactly friendly either. He comes into the living room and sits down on the big, fluffy armchair, still scrutinizing me. He pulls one ankle onto his opposite knee and settles into a position of authority. His dress shoe is a hard leather and shiny. And expensive looking. I'm in old jeans and a tee shirt. "Do you go to the Academy, Ashley?"

"No," I say too soft.

"What's that?" Man alive, this guy has an intimidating voice.

"She goes to the high school, Dad."

Mr. Williams looks at Erik. "How'd you meet?"

"She lives in the area," Erik says vaguely, but this only brings Mr. Williams' gaze back to me.

"In Stonehaven?"

I find my voice then. I refuse to be ashamed of where I live. "No, in Brookside," I say strongly.

"We met on the Greenbelt," Erik says, "and found out we both play. We've been practicing together some."

Mr. Williams looks at Erik. He seems composed, but there's a sharpness in his eyes.

"Just a few times," Erik adds.

"Well, it's nice to meet you, Ashley," he says, though it hasn't felt nice at all, "but it's probably time to get on home."

"Okay." I get off the bench, avoiding his eyes. I go to the couch to get my bag and feel like I'm intruding on his space even more. I slip on my Keds as unobtrusively as possible.

"I'll walk you out," Erik says and I give him a grateful look.

"She can see herself out," his dad says authoritatively. "You need to go up and change for the banquet. Your mother will be home any minute and she'll expect you to be ready to go."

There's a dawning look on Erik's face and I realize he remembers now why his dad is home. He gives me an apologetic look and heads for the stairs.

"Nice to meet you," I say to Erik's dad as I leave, but he doesn't reply. It's possible I said it too softly for him to hear. It's also possible he heard me just fine.

I step onto Erik's back patio and cross his yard, feeling like I'm sneaking away from the scene of a crime. By the time I get to the

Greenbelt, my hands are shaking. I hustle along, my legs feeling weak.

Well that was fun. God. That's Erik's dad?

My phone dings and I pull it out to see a text from Erik: I'm so sorry.

I stop on the Greenbelt and take a deep breath. I text him back: I don't think he likes me.

Erik: That's just how he is. Don't take it personally.

I take another deep breath. A jogger is coming down the path so I step to the side to make room. I'm not shaking any more, but I'm really not sure what to think about what just happened.

Erik again: Really. I told you before, he comes across hard at first.

Even after everything Erik's told me about his dad, I'm still a little stunned. I mean, I know his parents aren't exactly the warm and fuzzy type, but still. My parents would never be so rude to someone in their home.

Then again...

I think about how my dad might react if he came home to find me with a strange boy, never mind if he found us doing something indiscreet. I don't know that <u>politeness</u> would necessarily be my dad's first priority.

Maybe I shouldn't judge Erik's dad too harshly.

Me: <u>Okay.</u>

Erik: That's my dad. It's not me.

Me: So says Michael Corleone.

Erik: <u>Who?</u>

Me: Haven't you ever seen The Godfather?

Erik: <u>No.</u>

Me: We really need to get you up to speed.

Even though I'm still pretty shaken by my encounter with his father, it's helping me to keep things light. Besides, I don't want Erik to think I'm mad at him. He didn't do anything wrong.

Erik: Something to look forward to. :)

I smile.

Erik: Gotta get ready.

Me: K. Talk to you later.

I spend the evening lounging in the living room with my parents, instead of hanging out in my room like I might normally have done. It's a pretty uneventful night. My mom's reading, lifting her head from time to time to watch the news with my dad. I don't say much, but I'm comforted just being there and letting things feel normal for a while.

I consider talking to my mom about stuff. She's always been my confidant, but this is different. I don't want to talk to her about how physical things are getting with Erik. It's too private. I don't want to talk about what happened with Erik's dad, because then I'd have to fess up about how often we're there alone. Hell, we're <u>always </u>there alone.

Not for the first time, I think about what it must be like for Erik to be there by himself so much. My parents aren't necessarily <u>doing</u> anything for me right now, but they're here. It makes me sad to think how little of that Erik gets.

After dinner, I finally retreat to my room to do the bit of homework I have for history. Sitting cross-legged on my bed, I pull my binder out of my backpack. I find a piece of paper I've never seen before. It's an application for Music Fest.

I grab my phone and send off a text: When did you put this in my bag?

He responds immediately: When you went to the bathroom.

Me: Sneaky brat.

Erik: :) Fill it out.

I don't respond. Part of me knows he's right about all this. I say I'd love to be a pianist, but how can I do that if I never find the courage to get up on a stage?

Erik: Please.

I still don't respond. I put down my phone and fiddle with the end of my braid, staring at the application. Maybe I do just need to try it. Even if I don't do well, it'll help me get over my fear of playing in public. If that's all I accomplish, well, that's something at least. Right?

Erik: For me.

I sigh and grab my phone.

Me: No. But I'll do it for me.

Chapter 6

Over the next week, Erik and I focus most of our energy on practicing for Music Fest. We cool our jets a bit in the making-out department, and I ask him frequently when his parents will be home to be sure he isn't forgetting about anything. The last thing either one of us wants is another unpleasant surprise.

But by the time Music Fest rolls around, my bra gets undone with regularity and I've forgotten to be nervous about his dad. Instead I'm giving 100% of my nerves to the competition.

"Performance," Erik corrects me, whenever I refer to it as a competition.

It _is_ a competition, but for new players, like me, the focus is supposed to be on getting experience performing in a setting that's more formal than teachers' recitals tend to be. Not that I know anything about that either.

I don't tell my parents about any of this, for a couple of reasons. One, it'll just make the whole thing that much more scary. If they don't know, then it's not a big deal. It's almost like playing just for Erik.

At least, that's what I keep trying to tell myself to get over my nerves.

The second reason I don't tell them is for less honorable reasons: Erik's parents will be there. Of course, the one thing they take an interest in without fail is his "music career." That's how Erik and his parents talk about it: his music career.

Whereas I'm just a girl who's screwing around, in the end.

But if my parents go and see Erik, they'll want to talk to his parents and who knows what will get said. They think I see his folks all the time. They think Erik's parents must be delightful people, since he's "such a sweet boy"—my mom's words. My mom has been pestering us about meeting his folks. The longer this goes on, the worse I feel about sneaking around. But Erik and I are enjoying our freedom too much to willingly give it up.

When the big day arrives, Erik picks me up and drives us to the big church downtown where Music Fest will be taking place. We're there early for the preliminaries. Since I knew his parents wouldn't arrive until closer to start time, I didn't give the preliminaries much thought.

That was before I had to go into a little room and play in front of a panel of judges all by myself. I don't realize until after they announce who's going forward to the Honors Recital that I understand what the preliminaries were all about.

It seems so obvious in hindsight, and only demonstrates how out of my league I am. Yet, here I am, sitting with Erik in the rows of the nave reserved for the final performers. There's only two steps leading up to the front part of the church, the stage area. A rather intimidating black grand sits in the center. I'm distracting myself with the church's interior architecture and wondering how old the building is, because they don't make churches like this anymore.

Erik's keeping an eye out for his parents, and goes to say hello when they arrive. I stay put. We both know the day is coming that he needs to introduce me to them more formally, but today is not that day. Some other time we'll let them know Erik and I have moved beyond the "friend" stage they think we're in. I have enough going on to make me nervous without worrying about that.

I'm curling the ends of my hair around and around my finger. I've styled the hair on top in a braided crown with a slender braid that hangs down the back, but the rest of my hair is loose and wavy and kind of in the way. I'm wearing an orange summer skirt that looks fancier with the white heels I swiped from my mom's closet, and a plain white top. I'm pretty sure it's too late in the year for these light colors, but it was the best I could do. We don't have a whole lot of dress-wearing occasions in the Morrison household.

When Erik rejoins me, he takes my hand. "Hey, look at what you're doing to your finger!"

He unwraps my hair to reveal deep red marks around my left index finger.

"Keep that up and you'll cut off the circulation and won't be able to play."

"A valid excuse," I say, considering.

He takes my hand firmly in his. "You'll be fine."

I'd protest about him holding my hand knowing his parents are here, but I also know they can't see our hands from where they are. Besides, holding his hand is helping.

"Just remember to smile, bow, and don't look at the audience directly." He's already told me the trick to making it seem like you're looking at an audience even when you're not. You look just above the head of the person in the last row. It looks to them like you're looking at the audience, but you don't have to see them looking back at you with expressions that say, We think you're a big idiot.

Which is exactly how I feel right now. How did I let him talk me into this?

I look around at the other performers. They're all different ages and all wearing their Sunday best. Some of the male performers have button-down shirts and ties but a few, Erik included, are wearing suit coats.

That's something I didn't know about Erik before today: he's impossibly handsome in a suit coat. I wish we could skip the whole thing and just go make out somewhere, but since that's not an option...

"Hey, cut that out," he says softly, pulling my hand down from my mouth.

I didn't realize I'd started chewing on the end of my hair. Good lord, I haven't done that since I was a kid. I take a deep breath. I need to pull myself together.

"Ashley." His soft but firm tone draws my eyes to him. "You know your piece. Just play what you know."

"Okay." I take another deep breath and force myself to settle my nerves. I'm in this now, I may as well try to get through it the best that I can.

I scan the program again. Erik is about a quarter of the way down the list. I'm about a third of the way from the end. A thin man with balding hair but a distinguished presence goes up on the stage to welcome the audience and performers. After a surprisingly long acknowledgement of sponsors and helpers, the first performer is introduced and away we go.

There's no getting out now.

The first player is an adorable little girl I'd noticed during the preliminaries. She's wearing a pink poufy dress and a big bow in her hair. She can't be more than nine. She plays a surprisingly simple rendition and the audience claps when she's done. I don't know why I was expecting something more, but then, she's only nine.

The next performer is young, too, around twelve I'd guess, and he plays a more complicated number, but I suppose he's still showing his age. The third pianist looks to be closer to our age. I straighten in my seat expectantly. It's time to hear what the people my own age can do. His piece is certainly the most complex I've heard yet, but not near as complicated as I would have expected. Okay. So maybe I'm not the only seventeen-year-old beginner here after all.

The player right before Erik is also our age, and plays a piece closer to the complexity I expected to hear going into this. It's at least as complicated as the pieces we're playing, and truly sounds lovely. When he finishes, I lean over to Erik during the applause and whisper, "He's not as good as you."

Erik gives me a self-effacing grin, but it's true. I think he probably knows it. He's more than once accused me of not knowing my own talents, but whether that's true or not, I could never make the same accusation to Erik. His ear is too good for him to have any doubts about the quality of the music he creates.

It's his turn at last. As he gets on stage and settles in, I feel a swoop of nerves on his behalf. When he begins to play, I'm reminded of the first time I spied him through the windows of his house. He sounds brilliant, as he always does, but viewing him on stage adds an aura to the magic, just like watching him from afar did that day.

After listening to the other performers, and now listening to him, I know for certain what I've long suspected: Erik is in a class all his own.

Far, far above the rest of us.

It's the thing I love best about him.

When he finishes I leap to my feet, clapping enthusiastically. I'm not the only one. The audience rises in spurts. Maybe we're not supposed to give standing ovations at competitions, but I don't care. He faces the audience with a handsome smile, bows elegantly, and leaves a stage that feels far, far too small for the music he just played.

When he joins me, he's just Erik again, but that aura of greatness is still lingering about a bit. I'm in awe of him and want to give him a kiss right here in front of everybody. I have to settle for beaming at him. "That was fantastic!"

He smiles and takes my hand in his, giving it a squeeze.

As the program marches on—ever closer to my own name on the page—my nerves are growing, but I'm a little distracted by what I'm hearing. With only a few exceptions, the pianists our age aren't playing pieces nearly as advanced as what Erik and I chose.

After the latest such performance, I lean into him. "These songs aren't as hard as I thought they'd be."

He looks at me, a half smile on his face. "You're starting to see where you fit into the bigger picture, aren't you?"

I look back to the stage. I don't know about this. If I could've played a simpler piece I would have. I'm regretting playing something so complicated. Doesn't that just give me more opportunities to mess up? Why did he pick this? He should've known I could get away with something less demanding.

But before I know it, the time for thinking and worrying is past. The man in charge calls my name with ringing finality.

"Good luck," Erik whispers.

I rise from my seat, feeling like every eye in the house is on me. I climb the steps to the stage, but don't remember until I'm almost all the way to the piano to hitch a smile on my face. I get to the bench and turn to face the audience. I fix my eyes on the back wall and bow.

I sit down and look at the keys. It's the same as any other piano, when you get right down to it, but of course it's not the same. The sight of the black and ivory doesn't give me the same friendly feeling it usually does.

I just want to get this over with.

I only need to get through it, I tell myself firmly. That's what Erik's been telling me. That's all I have to do.

I put my hands on the keys and begin to play. I go measure to measure, watching my fingers as I go, and am kind of freaking out because I'm perfectly aware that I'm still here on the stage. I was counting on at least being able to slip down the rabbit hole and just lose myself in the music once I got started, but that's not happening. I have to think about every chord. I'm aware of every eye. But I keep going, because what the hell else am I going to do?

A third of the way through my piece, the music starts to rise and it's here that it finally, finally takes over. It's not me sitting at a piano performing anymore. I'm not just going through the motions. The music knocks its way through my nerves at last and my will surrenders.

Ah, here it is, I sigh as I allow the music to take me away. I escape the scrutiny of the audience gladly. This is my music now. It belongs to me. And I give it all the love and care it deserves.

I had doubted for a moment there, but now I know for sure: the music will always be there to save me.

I fly through the rest, carried on wings only I can see but everyone can hear. When I finish, I smile at the keys. My old friends.

A burst of applause claps over me like thunder and I look up abruptly. I forget to look at the back wall and instead look right at a sea of faces. My eyes land on a woman with an emerald green scarf around her neck, and I see it on her face. She's got that glow about her. She felt the music, just like I did.

How amazing, I think, still taking in this unexpected development.

I smile, stand, and bow. I see another face that wears an expression of being touched by music. And another.

The applause follows me off the stage. I'm not required to smile anymore, but I can't <u>stop</u> smiling.

Erik meets me and gives me an enthusiastic hug. "That was so great!"

"That <u>was!</u>" But I'm not talking about how I played. I'm talking about playing <u>up there.</u> In front of people. "I made them feel the music. <u>I</u> did that!"

He laughs and nods, like he understands. Of course, he does. I feel like I've been let into some sort of exclusive club. I had no idea how good this would feel.

We settle into our seats and even though my heart's still pounding, my body starts to relax. It's over. I did it. Erik takes my hand and I smile at him.

"Are you glad you came?"

I nod. "Thank you."

He smiles. "Don't thank me. You did it for you, remember?"

I grin. "I know, but I wouldn't have done it without you."

"Hmm," he says with a devilish look, turning back to the stage and squeezing my hand. "On to the next."

"What do you mean?"

The next performer starts to play and he puts his finger to his lips, still smiling.

When it comes time for the medallions to be presented to the winners, the emcee explains there are awards for each level.

"What does he mean 'level'?" I ask Erik, leaning close to him.

"It's like age categories, but for skill level instead."

"Oh, that's what that was?" I'd seen a question about levels on the application, but didn't know how to answer. Erik had told me he'd fill that in for me.

The emcee announces honorable mentions and winners for the first level. The winners are all young, under ten at least. The girl who wins honorable mention looks no more than eight. I'm again jealous of all these people who've had such a jump start on me. But it's not enough to kill my high. Even though I'm not winning anything, playing on stage in front of an audience has given me such a jolt it's still inside me, stirring me up.

I think about my fantasy of being a concert pianist. That wish, which has always been as vague and fuzzy as a wish on a star, is right now solidifying into something more real.

I've had a taste of that dream. I want it now, in a whole new way. I don't know how I'm going to make it happen, but as I sit here watching kids half my age climb on stage and get their awards, I'm feeling a level of determination I've never felt before.

That can't be the last time I get up on a stage.

I want to do that over and over again until the day I die.

As the emcee advances through the different levels, the winners are getting older, though there are the occasional standouts. "What level are you in?" I ask him. I want to know when to root for him.

The emcee announces there's one last group of awards, the highest level apparently.

"This one," Erik says, straightening in his seat.

I cross my fingers and grin at him. "First place, baby. Four times in a row."

He looks nervous, which I think is completely adorable, but he smiles at me. He can't seriously be nervous. There were some great pianists up there today, but no one touches Erik.

The emcee says there are three honorable mentions for this level, and starts rattling them off. When he gets to the last name, my mouth falls open: "Ashley Morrison."

The audience starts their polite clapping. Erik joins in, elbowing me. "Get up there."

I turn my disbelieving stare at him. "I thought this was your category!"

"Yours too!" He grins. "Get up there silly!"

I stand and make my way down the row feeling a bit numb. But then it hits me. When I get to the aisle I look at Erik and grin. Holy crap! It's all I can do not to run up to the stage.

They're already announcing the remaining winners as the assistant on stage presents me with a certificate.

At the top it says:

Idaho   Piano   Association Music   Fest Honorable Mention

Below that it reads:

Ashley Morrison.

Right there! I can't stop grinning like an idiot.

The emcee says, "And in first place," my breath catches in my throat, "Erik Williams."

I grin even wider and watch as he makes his way to the stage. He collects his medallion from the assistant, gives me a wink and a smile, and joins the line of winners. And me. I'm one of them! I don't even care that I don't get a medallion. Honorable Mention totally counts.

We all bow and start to exit the stage. Erik falls in next to me and we smile at each other. He looks so composed.

Half way down the aisle, I say, "Congratulations!"

"You too."

"Look!" I hold my certificate in front of him like a little kid showing her parents her kindergarten drawings.

He laughs. "Now do you believe me?"

"About what?"

"About how good you are."

I don't answer. I just grin down at my certificate. I can't say whether I believe him or not, even though something in me has shifted. I do feel more confident, no question about that, but it feels too new a thing to give voice to it. I don't want to chase it away.

I want it to settle inside me, and give me the courage to do whatever comes next.

Chapter 7

The following Wednesday, Erik and I are sitting on the floor in front of the couch, an ominous sheet of paper on the carpet in front of us. It's a print out of the admission requirements for the Juilliard School of Music.

I've admitted I want to try to be a concert pianist, and attending Juilliard would be a dream come true, but after looking at the list of requirements, I'm feeling more than doubtful about my chances.

For starters, there's the audition tape. I have to play a selection of three pretty advanced pieces for a minimum of 45 minutes, by memory. One has to be an etude by Chopin, one from a list of sonatas by the likes of Mozart and Schubert, and the last a "substantial composition" from a short list of classical composers. Though the thought of playing these for a Juilliard admissions board is more than intimidating, I already have enough pieces memorized to fulfill two of the three requirements.

It does not escape my notice that the piece Erik selected for me for Music Fest is one of them.

I'd only have to learn and memorize one more, which is a good thing since the deadline is only three and a half weeks away.

If that's all I had to do, it wouldn't be so bad, I guess. But there's this whole other list of requirements and one in particular is tripping me up: the artistic letter of recommendation. This is supposed to be from a teacher or coach who can speak to my musical abilities, discipline, and leadership. The whole thing just makes me feel ridiculous.

Erik's been trying to convince me to apply anyway. "You just write your essay explaining the situation so when they get your letters of recommendation, they can take that into consideration."

"Who's going to recommend me?" I don't think a letter from Erik is going to sway the admissions board.

Erik takes a deep breath. "Okay, listen. I've been telling Mr. Lamont about you and he's agreed to give you lessons."

"Erik, my parents can't afford—"

"He knows and he's not going to charge you."

"What?" As much as I've always wanted lessons, I don't think I like this. I don't want to be somebody's charity case. It must be written all over my face because Erik presses ahead, trying to reassure me.

"He <u>wants</u> to. He's been begging me to bring you in for a while now, but I knew you'd never agree so I didn't even bring it up. After he saw you play at Music Fest though..." Erik grins.

I'm softening in spite of myself.

"He said either I can bring you in or he'll show up here and wait for you."

My eyes widen and he shrugs.

"I don't think he'd actually stalk you, but he <u>really </u>wants to work with you before you go off to college. It wouldn't be for that long. He said he wants to talk to you first, but he'd probably be willing to write you a letter of recommendation."

I look over the list of requirements again. "I don't know. I think they're looking for people with more experience."

"You have it."

"I don't think <u>one</u> performance is quite what they have in mind."

"You won honorable mention in the highest level right out of the gate. Come on, you have to know how impressive that is. I say we frame you as a prodigy and let your audition do the rest."

Okay, that's what worries me. I'm willing to admit I have some natural talent, but we can't go overboard with the whole prodigy thing. Talented or not, there's no getting around the fact that I'm starting late and there's plenty, <u>plenty</u> of people in front of me.

I take a deep breath and look Erik right in the eyes. I'm calm, and firm. "Juilliard is the best school in the country. People like you from all over are going to be trying to get in. Only the best of the best are going to make that cut, Erik. They'd be stupid not to take you. You blew everyone out of the water on Saturday. But I'm not even the best of the best here in Boise. I'm sorry, but I don't stand a chance. I think I need to stick with BSU."

I've already been looking at colleges that might have music programs I can get into. I need to stay in state, to keep tuition low. That means Boise State. I have so much catching up to do, it's probably just as well.

Of course, there's the matter of the person sitting next to me and the likelihood that he will be heading to Juilliard in the fall. As if Juilliard weren't already the ultimate fantasy, Erik would only make it that much better. But I can't think about that now.

Erik sighs. "Look, you can apply to BSU too. But why not give Juilliard a shot? You can't just apply to one school anyway."

"You can't?"

"No. You have to have a safety school, at least. So BSU can be your safety school. With your GPA and SAT scores, there's no way you're not getting in."

He's probably right about that, but applying to colleges isn't cheap. At least, not when you live in a family where $100 is sometimes hard to scrape up. It seems foolish to waste my parents' money on a long shot.

"What's your safety school?" I ask him.

"Probably Hartman College."

"Hartman! That's some safety!"

He shrugs. "My parents want me to apply to the top ten conservatories. They figure at least one of them has to say yes. But Juilliard's the one we want."

"You're applying to <u>ten</u> schools?"

He cocks his head at me. "You know, you should apply to Hartman too, while you're at it. If you don't get into their conservatory, you can still go to the university side."

"I don't think I'm any more likely to get into Hartman's conservatory than Juilliard. And, look, I can't afford to apply to <u>three</u> schools."

"Two then. Hartman is your safety and Juilliard is where you're really going and then we can go together." He slips his hand around my waist and rests his forehead on mine. "Come on, baby. I was right about Music Fest. Give me some credit."

I smile. Yes, Music Fest was amazing. Fucking <u>amazing.</u>

"What do you have to lose?"

A reckless feeling takes flight in my chest. "Oh hell."

He breaks out into a grin and gives me a kiss so enthusiastic we end up falling back on the carpet. I start giggling. "I didn't say yes."

"Yes, you did." He's planting kisses all along my neck, "I heard you. We're going, baby, I just know it."

He comes up and kisses me, then leans on his elbow and grins down at me.

I'm smiling too. Maybe it's stupid, but he's right. I don't really have anything to lose by applying to Juilliard. I'll look into Hartman to see if I think that's a good idea or not.

"New York." Those brown eyes light up and his fingers lightly trail over my stomach. My body reacts instantly. "Can't you see us in New York together?"

"That would be incredible." I don't ask what will happen if he gets into Juilliard and

I don't. I'm not ready to think about that, and hell, if I'm going to apply, I may as well give it all I've got. "You really think your teacher will write a recommendation?"

Erik nods and says quietly. "He's bound to love you as much as I do."

My eyes widen but before I can respond he leans in and kisses me. And kisses me. And kisses me. Maybe he's afraid of what I might say to his confession, or maybe he has a hard time stopping these kind of kisses just like I do. I don't know, but when he finally comes up for air I put both hands on his face and lock eyes with him. "I love you, too."

It feels so strange to say that to someone I'm not related to, but I know it's true. I've known it for a while.

He gives me the most vulnerable smile. "You do?"

I nod and kiss him. And kiss him. And kiss him. It feels different than it has before. We've only just started, but I already know I don't want to stop this time. We've been so close to going all the way a few times now. After the last time, he even went out and bought a package of condoms so he'd be prepared when we're ready.

I don't know if he's ready. It's the first for him, too. But I'm almost certain I won't be the one putting the brakes on things today.

He's kissing me deeply, his hand up my shirt and under my bra. I have one leg hooked loosely around him. He starts kissing behind my ear and I shiver from the tingles he's giving me. "Let's go upstairs," I whisper.

It's not the first time we've moved a make out session to his bed. He kisses me again, then sits back on his knees, taking me by the hand. We get to our feet and jog up the stairs, casting glances out the window the whole way, to make sure we're not spotted by the rare passersby on the lawn.

As we cross the landing and head to his bedroom, I take out one of my braids. When we get to his room and he closes the door behind us, he helps with the last one. Something about making out with my hair down just adds to the whole thing. I know he likes it too because of the way his eyes get that burning look when he first sees my hair loose.

It's the same look he's giving me now. He puts both hands through my hair at the scalp, running his fingers down until he reaches my waist. He grabs my hips and pulls me to him, kissing me so expertly I've decided it's as natural a talent for him as playing the piano.

His erection presses against me and I return the pressure, holding him firmly around his lower back. There's too much material between us though, so we pause just long enough to slip off our jeans and tops. I'm only in my bra and underwear, and he's in his boxers. His length is straining against the material. The sight of it increases the heat of the blood coursing through my body even more.

He takes my hands and walks backwards, leading me toward the bed. I lay down with him willingly. We're on our sides, facing each other. I press my chest and stomach against his as his tongue dives into my mouth again. I wrap one leg around him. Now that there's so little fabric between us, the pressure of him against my mound is more intense.

I feel a little flutter of nerves, thinking about how far I want to go if he's willing, but I don't want to stop. In fact, the further along this goes, the more sure I am.

He unhooks my bra and we work together to slide it off and toss it aside. He rolls over on top of me and I wrap both legs around him. We grind against each other rhythmically. It still amazes me that such hardness against otherwise sensitive areas should feel so good, but it does. He feels amazing. He squeezes both my breasts, then leans down to take me into his mouth. I arch up to meet him. As he sucks and works my nipples, the heat and aching between my legs only increases.

I rub my hands over his firm back and shoulders. His sucking grows more intense, and I grab the back of his hair and push him into me. I'm panting heavily and trying not to moan too much, but sounds of pleasure escape me anyway.

He comes back up and we dive into a deep kiss, holding each other firmly. I run one hand down his back and slip under the band of his shorts so I can squeeze his bare ass. He cups one hand on my cheek, kisses me deeper, and thrusts his erection against me even harder.

He hits my clit just perfect, and a spike of pleasure zips through me. He thrusts me again, in the same spot, and we both moan. He does it again and I'm getting so shaky I wonder if it's possible to come just like this.

At this point, he lifts off me a bit, breathing hard. He has that heavy-lidded look that means he's as worked up as I am.

"If we're going to stop," he breathes, "we should probably stop."

"I don't want to stop."

He pulls back half an inch more, looking me right in the eye. I hold his gaze. Just looking at him makes my heart flip over. "Are you sure?"

I nod. "Unless you're not ready..."

Still breathing heavily, he looks at me for just a moment. Maybe he's not there yet. I'm careful not to let my disappointment show. He's never pushed me and I won't do that to him either.

"No, I want to."

I give him a shy smile. "You do?"

He nods and kisses me. My nerves kick up again. What if I do it wrong? But I haven't changed my mind. Maybe he's feeling something similar, because now that we've committed to it, there's a bit more hesitancy from both of us. But it doesn't last long. Soon we're groping and tasting each other's mouths and necks eagerly. He squeezes one breast and we angle our hips to press hard against each other.

Then I'm ready.

"Do you have a condom?" I whisper, even though I know he does. It seems the best way to say I want to start.

He pulls up, plants a firm kiss on my lips. "Hang on."

His bedroom has its own bathroom, just like the master at my parents' house, but he doesn't go in there. He starts digging around on a low shelf in his closet. I'm sure he's kept the package well hidden.

Watching him, I slide my panties off with faintly trembling hands. I drop them on the floor and wait with my legs slightly bent, knees together. I'm not sure how I should position myself. Should I be in a sexy position or something? But I stay how I am.

He must have found the box, because I hear the crumpling of a wrapper. He turns toward me, a little package in his hand, and stops when he sees me. I'm nervous for only a split second. Seeing the desire on his face sets me at ease.

Still taking me in, he pulls his boxers off and I see him for the first time. It seems I shouldn't stare, but I get a good look. I can't believe that's going to be inside me. I think he must be well-endowed, but with nothing to compare him to, I don't know for sure. I wonder if it's going to hurt or how it's going to feel, and these thoughts stir up my nerves a bit more. But the rest of me is still aching and ready and I can't wait for him to be in my arms again.

Our eyes meet and we smile at each other nervously. He comes closer to the bed, opening the package. I watch as he removes the condom and slides it down the length of his shaft. I wonder if I should be helping him. Is that the sexy thing to do? Maybe next time.

With his task completed, he climbs back onto the bed and gently settles himself on top of me. I love the way his weight feels on my body. "You still okay?" he asks, looking at me.

I nod. Holding his eyes, I give him a sensual kiss. This tips us both past some point we've never been before. He kisses me passionately. My body had cooled slightly while he'd taken care of the condom, but I'm hot everywhere again now. Every place he touches me, my skin feels on fire.

I hook my ankles around his thighs. I'm exposed to him in a way I've never been before. He reaches down and I feel the tip of his shaft against my folds. I hold my breath a moment, anticipating. He's searching, but hasn't quite found the right spot.

I reach down myself and take him in my hand. He lets me do the rest. I line up the tip with my entrance and whisper, "There."

My opening stretches as he starts to come in. I pull my hand away, grabbing his waist. He comes inside me slowly, stretching and filling me.

I gasp and he freezes. "Did I hurt you?"

I briefly shake my head no. <u>God no.</u> He pulls out slightly then slides inside me again, deeper this time. I exhale forcefully. <u>Oh god.</u> I'm wet everywhere, apparently, and the friction of his hard length along the inside of me feels so good I don't even know what to do.

The next moment, things break down as we try and fail to coordinate our movements. For a second I feel truly awkward because I really have no idea what I'm doing. Then we find a rhythm that I know is right because suddenly everything's clicking and I'm feeling a pleasure I can only describe as pure fire. He's sliding in and out of me and it all feels right. My legs spread wider of their own accord. He rocks on top of me and I wrap my arms around his back, gripping his firm shoulders.

He's panting hard and he's squeezing me harder. He almost seems to be in another world now. I've heard the first time goes quick for guys, so I'm kind of surprised he's not done already. I've also heard it's not always <u>there</u> for girls the first time, but as far as I can tell, everything's there for me. I

127

don't know what I was expecting, but I wasn't expecting this.

We're rocking together and he feels so good inside me I'm almost out of my mind. I'm moaning and sucking on his shoulder and neck and rocking my hips to meet him. The pleasure in my core is high and spiking higher.

I realize I'm about to come. My nerves at having an orgasm with Erik on top of me brings me back down a bit. His movements, however, suddenly grow faster and more intense. This new speed spikes me right back up there.

Before I have a chance to feel shy about anyone having an actual orgasm, he goes first. He groans deeply into the crook of my neck and his cock suddenly gets even harder. That pushes me over the edge so hard I couldn't fight it if I wanted to. I bite back the sounds I want to make but I can't stop my body from convulsing hard with him still thrusting me.

Bursts of pleasure spike inside me again and again. I realize I've cried out slightly without meaning to. I hang on to him firmly as everything comes to one last, sharp peak, then my body starts to slide back down.

Still pulsing with the after-effects, I come back to my senses and don't know what to think. I'm stunned by how high that pleasure was—by how goddamned good it felt—and I'm giddy from finally crossing this barrier from childhood into adulthood. And I'm a tiny bit vulnerable and embarrassed.

Still panting, we look at one another shyly, then laugh a bit. I feel better then. He gently pulls out of me and holds me close to him. I hug him back. I'm smiling widely.

Oh, I do love him.

I do.

We hold and lightly kiss one another only for a moment longer. "I need to take care of this," he says, lifting away from me. He gives me a wink as he gets to his knees and we both smile at each other. His expression changes, however, when he looks down at himself.

"Crap. It broke."

I get up on one elbow and look too. Sure enough. There he is, just him, without the thin rubber sheath over the tip. There's only a band of rolled rubber around the base.

Maybe I should be panicking more, but I'm not. I'm too busy being confused. "How did it break?"

"I don't know. Maybe I didn't put it on right?"

<u>Is there a wrong way to put it on?</u> "Maybe we should've Googled it."

We look at each other helplessly for a moment. I'm trying to remember when I had my last period and when women are supposed to be fertile. Hell if I know. Well, there's nothing to be done now.

"Well." I kind of shrug.

"God, I'm sorry."

"It's okay."

And that's the end of it. We quietly get dressed and he helps me do up my hair and we go back to the piano just like we always do. We only have time for a few more songs, then I head home. I greet my parents, wondering if they can see it on my face. But they say hi just like normal and we go about our evening. We have mom's famous stacked enchiladas with green sauce and I retire to my room and get started on my physics homework.

It's almost like I'm the same girl I was when I woke up this morning, even though I'm not. I'll never be that girl again, but that's okay. I like this new person I am now. She feels good.

I keep waiting to feel more scared about the broken condom, but it doesn't happen. Maybe because I figure the odds are with us. Maybe because I really am a stupid teenager, even though I hate it when adults use that phrase. I don't know what it is, but I have no desire to make myself more nervous than I am.

Eight days later, Erik has mastered the fine art of condom wearing, and we're forced to take a break from our new favorite activity because my period—blessedly—has finally started.

Chapter 8

By the time I've applied to colleges and am waiting for my letters—four months later—Erik and I are in so deep, the outcome of our applications carries a different weight than it did in the fall.

He's already received <u>five</u> acceptance letters, including one from Hartman, while I've only heard back from BSU. As expected, they let me in, so my safety school is in the bag. Come fall, at least I know I'll have <u>somewhere</u> to go. But Erik didn't apply to BSU and I wouldn't want him to go there even if he did. It's a good program but not of the same caliber as Juilliard, and not in New York, where someone of his talent really needs to be.

My parents agreed to pay for application fees to three schools. Erik may have considered Hartman a safety, but I didn't.

While I didn't worry about getting in on the academic side, I wouldn't have access to the music program if I wasn't accepted into their conservatory. At least at BSU I can participate in their music program, which isn't bad. But even I know that's not ideal, so in addition to coughing up the dough for Juilliard, we added Hartman College to the list. It's still a top ten school, so it feels like a long shot too. But, like Erik says, two shots are better than one. (I don't think he's counting BSU any more than I am.)

My dad is hoping for Hartman. Being in central California, it's not exactly close to Boise, but it's a lot closer than New York. My mom, who understands how badly Erik and I want to be together and how likely it is he'll be at Juilliard come fall whether I'm there or not, is pulling for that one just like I am.

I still don't know if she knows we're sexually active. As open as my mom can be about things, she's never brought it up and I haven't either. I've thought about asking her to take me to the doctor so I can get on some birth control, but I can't bring myself to do it. The issue of the pill is exactly what makes me think my mom is ignorant to the whole thing: I think she'd suggest the pill herself if she suspected. Do I really want to tell her that her little girl isn't so little anymore? And how would my dad react? Yeah. For now, Erik and I are sticking with condoms.

I'm almost certain his parents don't know we're having sex. I'm sure we'd hear all about it if they did. They're not too happy we're dating. His dad hasn't come out and said he thinks I'm beneath his son, but he's made it clear enough. Recently his mom told Erik she thinks I'm a distraction. If she only knew how much we really see of one another. She once told me not to get serious with Erik because his music career always comes first and after all, he'll be off to Juilliard in the fall. Neither one of us have heard from Juilliard yet, but she's made it obvious how she thinks it's all going to go down.

Juilliard has always been their top choice, but his parents have even more reason to want it now. His dad is up for a promotion that would mean relocating to New York City. Nothing's official yet, but it's looking good and they're making plans as if it were a done deal. If his dad gets it, he'll be off to New York in a few weeks, temporarily living in a condo provided by the company. Meanwhile, Erik and his mom would stay behind so he can finish the last couple months of school. She's already picked which movers will load everything up a few days after graduation and haul it across the country. Imagine paying people to pack up an entire house!

It's not that Erik necessarily <u>has</u> to go with them. In theory, he can go anywhere. But his family is one of those where the parents, in my opinion, have way too much say over stuff that should be his decision. Not that he wouldn't choose Juilliard anyway. Who wouldn't?

Erik doesn't seem to care whether his dad transfers to New York or not, because in his mind we're both already going to Juilliard. I don't know where he gets his confidence in me. I haven't heard from Juilliard <u>or</u> Hartman. What if I don't get into either one?

For the few weeks I've been working with Mr. Lamont, which has been freaking incredible, I've learned a lot. I keep wishing I could re-do my audition tapes, but it's too late for that. All I can do is hope for the best and wait, and wait, and wait.

It's Friday afternoon and I'm walking home from school, approaching my house. Erik's picking me up in a few minutes for our date. I'm looking forward to it, but at this precise moment, my mind is focused on one thing and one thing only. I hitch my school bag higher on my shoulder and head straight to our mailbox, just as I have every day for weeks. And just like every other day, I get a swoop of anticipation in my stomach when I pull out the daily stack of mail.

Flipping through, I freeze when I see a cream-colored envelope from Hartman College. My heart starts banging around in my chest.

Something! Finally!

But I just stand there gawking at it. The maroon crest is embossed on the upper left-hand corner. It's a thick envelope. That has to be a good sign, right? I got all kinds of paperwork with my acceptance letter to BSU and Erik's have been the same way. But if Hartman were going to tell me to take a hike, how many pages would they really need? I walk up the sidewalk, still studying the envelope. I unlock the front door, drop my bag on the floor, head for the kitchen, and toss the remaining mail on the counter.

Missy, our cat, is lounging on the bench under the kitchen window. She looks nice and toasty in her little spot of sunshine and blinks at me languidly.

I squeeze the envelope, trying to guess how many pages are inside. Five maybe? I think about waiting for Erik for moral support—he should be here any time now—but I have a feeling I know what this is going to say. All of a sudden, I can't wait another second to find out for sure.

Holding my breath, I rip into the envelope and pull out a stack of neatly folded pages.

Three seconds later, I'm screaming and jumping around in the kitchen, and Missy is bolting down the hallway in terror.

The doorbell rings and I run for the front door, knowing who it is. I fling it open to see Erik's startled face. "I got into Hartman! I got into Hartman!"

He whoops and hangs onto me as I launch myself at him, wrapping my arms and legs around him. "I got in! I got in!"

He laughs and spins me around. "I knew you would, baby!"

I drop to my feet and show him the letter. "Look! Look at it!"

He puts his arm around me and squeezes my shoulders. I lean against his chest, grinning at the letter. Then I start flipping through the other pages. It's all there: the admissions form and information about deadlines and fees. The fees scare the hell out of me, frankly, but I've applied for scholarships and aid at all three schools and can only hope for the best. If I have to, I'll work part-time to help pay for things and take out loans for the rest.

"I can't believe it." I exhale sharply. "Hartman. I can't believe I got in."

"See?" Erik says with his trademark confidence. I already know what he's going to say next. "I told you you're good enough. Now Juilliard doesn't seem like such a stretch, does it?"

I look up at him. He's grinning down at me. I smile broadly. God, he's right. For the first time, Juilliard really, truly feels like it could happen. If I could get into Hartman...

"I love you."

He smiles. "I love you too, sweetheart." He wags his eyebrows at me. "Time to celebrate?"

"My parents will be home soon," I say, laughing lightly and returning my attention to the letter. I hold it to my chest. I can't believe I got in to freaking Hartman.

"Well, how long does it take?" He pinches my ass.

It's tempting, I have to admit. But I settle for giving him an enthusiastic kiss. We hold each other tightly. I think he's as excited about this new development as I am.

New York. Come fall Erik and I could really be together in New York, studying at one of the best music conservatories in the country.

"Ready for the fair?" he asks, when we finally come up for air.

I smile. I'm ready for anything with him.

We should've just gone back to his place to get things out of our system, but we'd probably still be groping each other on the Ferris wheel and ducking into nooks to steal a kiss. We can't ever seem to get enough of each other. No matter what else we're doing—playing, talking, watching movies, or spinning around on wild rides at the fair—it never seems to be too long before we're going at it to one degree or another.

After hitting our favorite rides (we went on the drop tower five times), we climb into his car and head home.

Well, kind of home. The roundabout way to home. The way that includes a stop at a secluded park we discovered a couple months ago. It's since become "our spot" during those times when the privacy of his home is unavailable. All it takes is for us to pull into the darkened parking lot and I start to get wet. Expecting this was probably where we'd end up tonight, I even wore a denim skirt for the occasion.

Erik loves it when I wear skirts.

He kills the engine and looks over at me with a delicious grin. "Hello future Juilliard student," he says in a sultry voice.

"Don't curse it." I grin.

He leans over and puts his hand on my bare knee, gently cupping the inside of my leg. I lean in too, his hand sliding up my inner thigh as we come together for a sensual kiss. God, can he kiss. His lips lure me in and raise my body temperature as much as anything he does with his hands.

Not that I overlook what he does with his hands. His fingers trail softly up the gap in my thighs. I spread my legs slightly, anticipating his touch.

I glance around the park to make sure we're still alone, even though we always are. Still, we tend to move quick here, just in case. Not that my body needs it. It seems I'm always ready for him, whether he spends the time on foreplay or not.

As he works his way up my inner thighs, I reach for him too. Two can play this game. When I find him, I squeeze his hard shaft under the thick fabric of his jeans and make him groan.

His fingertips reach the top of my thigh, making the tender skin there tremble. He expertly tucks his fingers underneath the fabric of my panties and dips into me to get my moisture. I exhale shakily and his mouth starts moving down my neck, suckling on my skin along the way. His wet fingertips slide over my hard bud and I moan.

Rubbing his slick fingers over me, he leaves my neck and bends down toward my mound. Taking one last glance around, I lean the seat back and rearrange to give him better access. Head between my legs, he pulls back the crotch of my panties and starts to lick me. No longer able to reach his cock, I settle for grabbing his hair and rocking my hips.

His hands firmly rub up my inner thighs, spreading me further and gently pressing my knees open. I'm panting and trying not to make any noise. Even though I find the risk of the park exciting, I'm not going to tempt fate by being loud. But the way he's working me is sending me into that place that isn't as cautious as it should be.

"Erik," I whisper, pushing his head harder into me and arching my hips up more. "God, yes."

He slides one hand under my shirt and pulls my bra aside so he can fondle my bare nipple.

I spread myself as much as I can. The restrictive space in the car only seems to heighten my pleasure as I long to open wider but am hemmed in. I'm so wet I can feel the juices coming out of me. He dips his tongue down to lap it up and I tremble with the unexpected pleasure of it. He returns to my swollen bud, bringing me closer and closer to the edge.

Still squeezing my breast with one hand, he slides a finger inside me and bends it against my wall. That gives me a shock of ecstasy so sharp, my whole body curls hard inward and I'm forced to stifle a cry.

Then another. And another as he works now two fingers inside me. My legs begin to tremble then my body bursts into an orgasm. I let out an extended, muffled whimper as I contract again and again. Pleasure bursts outward from my core in powerful waves. I throw my head back against the seat and arch my back. Even though I'm thrashing a bit, his mouth stays right with me.

He stretches my orgasm out for so long I almost think I can't take it anymore. He lifts up and pulls out his fingers quickly. He's learned this abrupt ending only makes me want it all over again, but this time with his cock.

Tonight is no exception. My core starts to ache.

His eyes meet mine and we watch each other hungrily as he sits back in his seat to release his bulging dick from his pants. He glances around, checking to make sure the coast is still clear, and I slide my panties off. He opens the glove box to retrieve a condom from his stash there.

"Fuck."

I raise my eyebrows. "Don't tell me we're out." But now I remember the last time we were here, we'd used the last one.

His head drops. "Shit."

Yeah, that's about how I feel. I want him inside me so badly I can't hardly think straight. "Just pull out early." I tug on his shoulder. "Come on."

We've done that before, and even though we both know sperm can be present before a guy ejaculates, it's only a tiny bit and this has always worked for us in the past. It's not the first time we've had to improvise. We both like it better when he can come inside me, but it's better than nothing. Besides, it feels so good when it's just him. If I'm judging him correctly, he doesn't want to wait any more than I do.

Sure enough, he closes the glove box firmly and starts to climb on. We arrange ourselves quickly, well knowing how to make things work in his car, and before I know it, he's pounding me eagerly. If anyone were to walk by, there'd be no hiding his bare ass and my feet in the air, but I don't care. I'm so hot for him and he's so hard for me, I know we won't be in such a compromising position for long.

145

I grab his tight ass and squeeze him firmly as he rams his shaft into my wet center.

"That's right baby," he whispers thickly. His breath is hot on my ear. "Take that cock."

The ecstasy growing between my legs only intensifies when he talks to me like that. I'm already nearing my peak. As he thrusts me, his pelvis hits my clit. I get that burst of pleasure at the same time he's deep and full in me. I angle up to meet him just a bit more and now his sack is hitting my anus. With the entire area down there flooded with pleasure, I'm almost going over again.

"I'm so close," he says. I already know. His cock is reaching its peak of hardness and stretching me completely.

"Me too," I gasp out, and then with two more powerful thrusts and slaps of pleasure on every part of me I could want touched, I'm done for. I tuck my head into his neck and cry out as I climax again. I try to soften my cries but he's continuing to come at me and I'm in a frenzy. I contract around his hard shaft, and my body convulses with ecstasy. I dig my nails slightly into his back and he groans with the pleasure of it. I realize I'm not helping him hold off until I'm done. He manages it though.

I ride wave after wave, and at last I start to release and come back down. Only when my aftershocks are done and I'm starting to feel the glow of satisfaction does he pull out in a rush. I quickly grab the head of his cock just as he spills all over the seat. Thank god they're leather. I stroke him firmly, loving the feel of him pulsing in my hand and the sound of his deep groans rumbling in my ear.

When it's over and he drops his weight on me, I kiss his cheek and hold him tightly. He kisses my collarbone tenderly. "I love you, Ashley."

"I love you, too." I lightly slap his bare cheek. "And your sexy ass."

He laughs and gives me one last kiss before we clean up, put ourselves together, and finally head for home.

A couple weeks later, I slowly cross Erik's backyard, listening to him improvise on the piano. We started improvising a few months back, when on impulse I played a song that had been lilting around in my head. I'd done that several times on the piano at school, but only when I was alone. There always seems to be some sort of song in my head, my own "compositions" Erik calls them. Maybe, maybe not. In any case, the first time I improvised in front of him, he'd been stunned to hear me come up with something so nice on the fly. He got really excited and started praising me in that crazy way that makes me feel uncomfortable, just like when he saw me sight read for the first time. I don't know why that kind of thing makes me mad. I really don't. But he backed off quickly.

Anyway, it's not a big deal, because when he tried it, we discovered he wasn't bad at improvising either. He seems to struggle with it on his own for some reason. I hear that fumbling in the song he's playing now. But when we play together, we somehow feed off of each other and it all seems to click.

Thinking about that connection we have, even when we're both at the keyboard, only makes me dread what's coming even more. I've had the sick tingling of it the whole way here.

I climb the steps to the patio, let myself in through the back door, and quietly close it behind me.

I come around the corner and set my bag on the big, overstuffed chair. I don't sit down though. I just stand there, watching him and feeling afraid.

He's been lost in his music, and just now notices me. He glances at me, smiles, goes back to the keyboard, then does a double take on my face. He stops and slides off the bench. "What's wrong?"

As he comes over, I reach into my bag and withdraw the envelope that came in the mail today.

The Juilliard School of Music is in bold type in the return address. The envelope is unopened, and ominously thin.

I'm clearly not the only one who thinks things already don't look good, because Erik stops when he sees it. "When did you get this?" he asks soberly.

"Today."

He's had his acceptance letter from Juilliard for a couple weeks now. Every day that's gone by has made me more and more nervous, especially since his dad got the promotion and is set to leave for New York in another week. As we've waited for the word from Juilliard, Erik's confidence in me hasn't waned at all. This is the first I've seen him look scared about it. I've asked him before what will happen with us if I didn't get in. He's only ever said, "You will."

The envelope from Juilliard is trembling slightly in my hand. I hold it out further. "You do it."

He takes it without a word. I watch as he opens the envelope, withdraws the letter, and communicates with the expression on his face what I already suspected. My dream of going to Juilliard was just that: a dream. And it's over.

All of a sudden, I can't stay.

"Okay." I grab my bag and hitch it back on my shoulder.

"I don't get it." He's still staring at the letter in disbelief. I feel a bittersweet wave of love for him. He really did believe I'd get in. How will I survive losing him?

"I'll talk to you later." I give him a peck on the cheek.

"You're going?"

I nod and turn away from him, heading for the back door.

"Ashley, wait." He starts to follow me.

"Erik, I just want to be alone, okay?" I open the door.

"But—"

Still standing in the doorway, I face him briefly. "Please," I say. "Stay here."

He blinks at me, giving me a pained expression.

That's the moment my heart starts to break wide open. I can't stand it. I turn away and cross his yard alone. I feel him watching me, but I don't look back. I manage to hold in the tears until I get to the Greenbelt, and then it's all over. I don't want to cry here either—I'm bound to encounter other people between here and home—but I can't help it.

I'm not going to Juilliard. I can't believe I ever seriously thought I had a chance anyway. Who was I kidding? Kids there have years and years of training and experience, while I've been fumbling around just trying to catch up. Why did I let Erik convince me I had a chance? The person who's in love with you doesn't exactly have the most unbiased opinion.

The thought of Erik being in love with me only gets me crying harder. A jogger up ahead is drawing near, so I furiously brush my tears away and try to look normal. But my heart aches so much I think it's literally going to break. Who knew the expression of a broken heart wasn't just an exaggeration?

Erik loves me. I know this. But there's no way he's passing up Juilliard. Even if he wanted to (would he want to?), his parents would never allow it, not with everything Juilliard has to offer, being right there in the heart of New York City. The decision was made the second he got his acceptance letter. The fact that his parents are moving there only sweetened the deal.

Knowing I'd gotten into Hartman, his mom even said right in front of me, "Juilliard is your future, Erik. Your father and I won't pay a dime for you to go anywhere else."

Maybe she's not so oblivious to us after all, if she felt she had to make a threat like that.

My phone dings and I pull it out of my pocket.

Erik: Are you mad at me?

Me: <u>No.</u>

I just need to be alone. I can't talk to him right now. I turn off my phone and put it back.

God. What am I going to do now?

When I break the news to my parents, I can only stand so much of their efforts to cheer me up before I head to my room. I really don't want to hear my dad talking about what an accomplishment it was to get into Hartman. I don't want to hear my mom saying maybe Erik and I can wait for each other. I don't want to hear any of it, because it's all bullshit.

All of it.

I don't know if I can bring myself to go to Hartman. I'd only get there and fumble around and they'd realize letting me in was a mistake. How am I supposed to keep up with the other students at a school like that? It's a joke. I'd be better off at BSU and it'd be less expensive too. And since Erik is going to be at Juilliard where he belongs anyway, what difference does it make where I end up?

I'm lying on my bed, fully dressed, watching the room get dark as the sun sets. It suits my mood just fine. My mind is swirling with darkness. I've never been in such a black, hopeless state before, and I feel it swallowing me whole.

I'm too despondent to stop it.

Until one thought comes out of nowhere. It hits me with such sharpness that I suck in a breath and hold it.

I stare wide-eyed at the ceiling, my blood pounding through my entire body.

Filled with dread, I slowly sit up and open my nightstand drawer.

I have a horrible feeling things are about to get much, much worse.

Chapter 9

It's past eleven-thirty when there's a soft knock on my window. Even though Erik's never come to my window before, I know it's him. I get off my bed, where I've been lying fully dressed for some time now, and pull back the drapes to reveal his face.

I don't know if I'm ready for this.

I open the window and he comes right in, as if it's the most normal thing in the world. "Why haven't you answered my texts?"

"I turned off my phone."

He looks pretty worn, but he's also smiling and his eyes are lit up. Before I even have a chance to wonder what's going on, he says, "I just had it out with my parents. I told them I'm going to Hartman."

I blink at him. "You... what?"

He smiles and nods and brings me into his arms. I'm swirling with his news. Hell,

I've been swirling with news all day. "They agreed to that?"

"I'm an adult." His voice carries a hint of the rebellious tone I can imagine he used with his parents. Honestly, I can't imagine standing up to either one of them. "I can go where I want. I don't care if they won't pay for it. I'm so sick of them trying to control me with money, anyway."

My cheek is against his chest and I'm in his arms, but none of that is enough to chase away the horrible fear that's so big inside me. "Why are you doing this?" I ask stupidly. As if I don't know. But... I know something he doesn't.

He pulls back to look at me, holding me by both shoulders. "For you, silly," he says with a smile, but he frowns when he sees my face. "Don't you... want us to be together?"

I sigh. "Erik..." I hate the look of confusion and fear I see on his face. He thinks I'm going to reject him. He has no idea how much worse it is.

I push through my hesitancy and spit it out: "I'm pregnant."

And there it is. The cold fear I've been feeling for the past hour spreads over his face. He slowly drops his hands.

With that one movement, it seems he's telling me the one thing I fear the most: I'm on my own.

"What? Are you sure?"

I fold my arms in front of my chest and retreat to my nightstand. I open the drawer where I hid a pregnancy test months ago. I'd had a scare then too, which turned out to be nothing. The drug store had a sale on the double pack of test kits. Since it was cheaper than buying just one, I went ahead and got the package of two. The unused one had been buried deep in my drawer, forgotten until earlier this evening when I'd been lying on my bed and suddenly realized how far past my cycle I was. I guess I'd been too worried about waiting for the goddamned letter from Juilliard to pay much attention.

The test stick is resting on the opened package inside the drawer. I take it out and hand it to him. I have to reach, because I don't want to get too close to him. This is the kind of thing that makes boys cut and run, isn't it? Especially rich boys with parents who've warned him about slumming with a girl like me. They probably think I'm just the type to go and get knocked up.

And guess what? They're right. The fact that I can't really play the piano after all is irrelevant. Whether I keep the baby or give it up for adoption, I can't very well be giving birth in the middle of my first year of college, can I?

I won't even consider abortion, and will hate Erik forever if he suggests it.

He takes the stick and looks down at the double pink lines. His hands are shaking. "Do two lines mean..." He doesn't finish.

I exhale sharply and take the package out of the drawer, flipping it over so he can see for himself.

Two lines mean I'm fucked.

Holding both the test and the empty box, he stumbles over to the bed and sits down heavily. I step back, giving him space.

I didn't expect to feel like this with him here. I didn't expect to feel so alone in this, and so scared of his reaction. But there it is.

"Sweetheart," he says softly, then looks up at me. "What do you want to do?"

"What do I want to do?" I say, more harshly than I meant to. "Glad to know you think this is my problem."

"No!" He jumps to his feet and comes toward me but I step back, holding up one hand. He stops, glancing at my raised hand, then looks at me earnestly. "I didn't mean it that way. I just... wanted to know what you want to do. I mean, are you wanting to... keep it or—"

"Don't you dare tell me to get an abortion!" I say loudly.

He startles and holds up his hands. "I wasn't—"

But I can't think straight. My blood is pulsing through my body and rushing through my ears. My entire future is falling away from me. The piano. Erik. Everything. Now that he's here, I can't bear the thought of hearing him say I'm on my own. "I'm not getting a fucking abortion," I spit. "You don't get off that easy."

"Hey!" His voice is sharp now, too. "I didn't say—"

My bedroom door flies open. Erik throws everything in the drawer and closes it quickly and we turn to see my mom standing there.

"What's going on?" She's using her mom voice. "Erik, what are you doing here?"

"He was just leaving," I say, without looking at him.

"Ashley," he says, softer now but still firm, "we need to talk about this."

"Later." I can't handle this. I can't handle any of this. I want to throw myself in my mother's arms like the child I apparently still am and have her fix everything for me. How could I let this happen?

"Talk about what?" my mother asks.

My dad appears in the hallway behind her. "Erik? When did you get here?"

I sit at the foot of my bed, crossing my arms and keeping my head turned away from him. I need him to leave, and I need my dad to go away. I just need my mom.

And that's exactly what happens. Erik apologizes and excuses himself and leaves in a rush, this time out the front door. My mom softly says to my dad, "Let me talk to her," and he goes away too. When she comes in

161

and closes the door behind her, my hands fly to my face and I start to cry.

God, how could I be a mother? I'm still a kid myself.

My mom doesn't come to me right away though. She hovers at the door just for a moment, then she goes to my nightstand drawer. I don't try to stop her. I hear the drawer open, and she exhales.

"Oh, Ashley."

"I'm sorry mom," I cry into my hands. "I'm sorry."

She drops on the bed next to me, pulls me into her arms, and I sob helplessly on her chest.

A good hour later, my mom finally leaves my room. We've both agreed she'll tell my dad herself. I lay on my bed, curled on my side, dreading things once more. What's going to happen to me?

It isn't long when I hear raised voices. I pinch my eyes closed and press my closed fists against my forehead. I hear a sharp knock on our front door and my heart freezes. Oh God, please don't let that be Erik. Not now.

But the new voice I hear coming from the living room doesn't belong to Erik. I scramble off my bed and hurry down the hallway toward the angry male voices talking over one another. I go into the living room to see Erik's dad facing off against mine and looking larger than ever. My mother is there too, looking like she's trying to diffuse things.

"You don't get to come into my house and demand things," my father is saying.

"What you do with your daughter is your business," Erik's dad says in that big voice of his, "but what I do with my son is mine. He has a future and I'm not going to let this ruin it."

"Oh, my daughter doesn't have a future?"

"I'll give you two weeks," Mr. Williams says, apparently not feeling it worthwhile to answer my dad's question.

"Get out of my house."

"Gladly." Mr. Williams manages to give a dismissive look to our home, my parents, and me, all in one fell swoop. "Before I go, let me make things clear for you. Your daughter's eighteen, correct?"

"She just turned eighteen in January," my dad says impatiently. "What of it?"

"Well, my son is still seventeen. I can press charges against her for having sexual relations with a minor."

Just when I thought I couldn't be more terrified of my own future, Erik's dad proves me wrong. He doesn't look like he's making an idle threat either. Being a lawyer, he'd know just how to do it, too.

"Be reasonable," my dad says angrily. "You know it's not like that with these kids."

"Don't I? She clearly has no regard for his parents' wishes. I specifically forbade them from being together and she did what she wanted with my son anyway."

I feel slapped. He forbid us? When did he do this? My mind rapidly works backwards. I realize I haven't seen his parents since Erik got his letter from Juilliard and his mom made the comment about not paying for him to go anywhere else. Is that when they told him? Was he hiding that from me, or is his dad bluffing now?

He doesn't look like he's bluffing. He looks pissed that his direct orders have not been obeyed.

My dad simply looks stunned.

"Oh, you didn't know about that?" Mr. Williams says smugly. "Why am I not surprised? Why don't you try reigning in your daughter a little better?" He exhales dismissively. "I'm done here. She can get rid of it or I can have her convicted of being a sexual predator." He pulls out his wallet, oblivious to my dad straightening and puffing his chest.

"Are you threatening my daughter?"

"If you don't have the money for an abortion, I'll pay for it." He tosses his business card on the couch and gives my dad a hard look. "Let me know when it's done."

He turns to leave and I think my dad is going to launch himself at him, but my mom grabs his arm urgently. "Don't!"

Mr. Williams leaves and the front door slams. My dad is huffing like a bull. That

165

scares me as much as anything. I've never seen my dad like this. I've never seen anything like this. I've never cared much for Erik's dad, but I can't believe he just did this.

My dad storms to the door and pounds it hard with his open hand. "Fucking asshole!"

I startle, blinking at him.

"Those people think they own everybody." He spins and his eyes land on me. I cringe and step back.

"Get to your room," he says calmly, but he's still panting like an animal ready to strike.

"Robert—"

He holds up one finger, silencing my mother. His eyes stay on me. "I'm disappointed in you, Ashley. Get out of my sight."

Chapter 10

The next day, I decide I'm not up to going to school. My parents don't push it. They both talked to me this morning, and my dad has softened since last night. He apologized for his harshness, gave me a hug, and said we'd all get through it together. I tearfully asked him if I'd have to get an abortion and he assured me I wouldn't have to do anything I didn't want to do.

"What about what Mr. Williams said?"

"We'll figure it out. He probably wasn't feeling any more reasonable about things last night than I was. I'll give it a couple days and then talk to him."

I didn't turn on my phone until my parents left for work. After listening to the litany of alerts as it got caught up, I read the many texts from Erik, beginning with one he sent me when I was still walking home from his house.

Erik: It's going to be okay.

He meant the Juilliard thing, which seems so long ago and far away now.

There were a few more texts after that, asking if I was all right, then there was a long break. He didn't send the next text until evening: <u>I have something to tell you. Something good.</u>

I assume that was after he'd confronted his parents about Hartman. I can only imagine how that went. Erik may have thought he was going to do what he wanted to do, but after witnessing his dad last night, I doubt they were going down without a fight.

Then there were a series of texts—<u>Please text or call me,</u> and <u>I really need to talk to you,</u> and <u>Can I come over?</u>—which must have all been before he came to talk to me.

His last text was sent right after he left here last night: You won't be alone in this. I promise. I'm here for you, Ashley. I love you.

Maybe our fathers weren't the only ones who didn't know how to handle things last night. After thinking back on Erik's reaction, I see he didn't really say anything to indicate he was abandoning me. He was just taking it all in, and trying to find out my thoughts about the matter.

Tearfully, I sent him a belated reply: Thank you. Can I come over after school today? I love you too. I'm so scared.

But that was six hours ago, and I haven't heard a word.

An hour after the time his school would have let out, I take a chance. I don't have long before my parents get home, so it's now or never. I walk along the Greenbelt and to Erik's house, wondering what I'll find when I get there. What if his parents are home? What if he's home, but doesn't want to see me?

I try not to think that. I try to have faith in his last text. But after so much radio silence, it's hard.

When I get to his house, no one's home. I don't bother texting. This time, I call.

It goes straight to voice mail. I listen to his recording instructing me to leave a message—my heart aching at the sound of his voice—but I hang up.

I walk home with my arms wrapped around myself, shivering the whole way.

A couple days go by and I go through the motions at school. I don't tell a soul. Graduation is in two months, so I won't really be showing too much at that point. I'd rather not be <u>that girl</u> so I just keep my mouth shut.

Erik hasn't texted or called me (in fact, his number is out of service, which is freaking me out), but his dad has been pestering my dad, wanting to know if "things have been taken care of." We've decided I'll put the baby up for adoption, but apparently Erik's dad is still being too threatening for my dad to want to say so.

I let four whole days go by before I storm over there. I know his dad is due to leave for

New York soon, and I'm determined to give both Erik and his dad a piece of my mind. But they have the upper hand once again. The house is closed up and there's a For Sale sign out front.

This knocks the wind out of me. Did they decide to move early? But... what about Erik finishing school? Is he all the way to New York at this very moment?

Fuck. Goddamn him.

The anger I'd been carefully nurturing all week dissolves into shaking and tears.

That's when I hate him. Just like that.

When I get home and tell my parents, my dad gets a stony look on his face.

We're at the kitchen table. My dad is standing, seeming too tense to sit, but mom is next to me rubbing my back. I'm scowling at the old candle centerpiece in the middle of the table, leaning on my arms and balling my hands into fists.

"They'll go to any lengths," my dad says, "won't they? I thought maybe his father was just blowing hot air about pressing charges against you, but I'm not so sure now."

171

Clearly, he's even more skittish about telling Erik's dad I won't be getting an abortion.

I'm past caring.

"Lie about it then," I say furiously. "They can both kiss my ass."

Neither one of them correct my language. "Honey, I understand being upset." My mom rubs my back gently. "I am too. But... I don't know how angry I am at Erik. I have a feeling his dad is putting a lot of pressure on him."

But I don't care what his reasons are.

I'll never forgive him for leaving me the way he has.

Two weeks later, I've had my first appointment with the doctor, who confirmed I'm almost five weeks along. My parents are still trying to figure out how to handle things with Erik's dad. I oscillate between furiously hating Erik and missing him so much I think I'm going to die. Sometimes I find myself going through all sorts of scenarios in my head, giving Erik the benefit of the doubt. What if his dad is threatening him too? But in the end my hurt at being abandoned is too much to overcome. If he really loved me, wouldn't Erik at least try to talk to me? What excuse could he have for that?

One last thing is contributing to my feeling that I'm in a downward spiral: I haven't touched a piano since it happened. I could go back to the school one, and probably should, but I can't. Everything is too black and heavy.

I can't even hear music in my head.

I've taken to walking along the Greenbelt again, mainly because I just want to get away all the time and I have nowhere else to go. I walk in the opposite direction of Erik's house though.

One day, in the middle of May, I'm a good mile and a half from the house when the cramping starts. It's the thing that makes me turn back toward the house much earlier than I would have. I feel like I just need to lie down.

By the time I get home, I'm in horrible pain and know something's terribly wrong. The dull cramping I felt at first has steadily worsened. There's a sharp, hot pulling sensation in my uterus and I can't walk upright. My dad isn't home yet, but as soon as Mom sees me, she rushes to my side.

I tell her what's happening and she loads me into the car. I wonder if I'm losing the baby. I'm in too much pain to worry much about the confusing fact that I both do and do not want to have a miscarriage.

But, like everything else these days, it's out of my hands.

We get to the hospital and they confirm I'm miscarrying. They end up putting me under for a D&C—a common procedure to scrape my uterus since I'm not miscarrying cleanly, which scares me to death—and I wake up an hour later with my parents by my side. I'm no longer pregnant. I'm no longer in pain.

I'm ultimately relieved.

But I can't bring myself to admit that to anyone.

And I have no idea what to do about the big, gaping gash in my heart where Erik used to be.

I returned to my piano not long after that and ended up going to Hartman after all. Between scholarships and grants, my costs were just barely covered. That first year in college, though, was all about trying to fill the big Erik-sized gash in my heart, and really not knowing how to do it. I could escape into my music some, but even that wasn't enough. Aside from struggling that first year to keep up with all those well-trained musicians, Erik had become infused in my music and I didn't yet know how to exorcise him.

I went a little wild, as I suppose many freshman do, but for me it was far more wildness than was good for me. The parties were fun, but both the drinking and the guys tended to get out of hand. I'd push myself past my comfort zone. Looking back on that time in my life, I think I was trying to punish myself for something, but I'm still not sure what. It wasn't that I was sleeping with a ton of guys, but the guys I slept with meant nothing to me, and having sex with them always made me feel miserable.

Which is sort of why I was doing it.

Surprisingly, it was Sam who cured me of it. Sam, my tiny little firecracker of a friend, who seemed to consider a night of casual sex as both the best possible form of recreation, and the cure for just about any ailment.

It came about when I stopped by Sam's room in her dorm to pick her up for a frat party. Chloe and Isabella weren't able to come to this one and Sam's roommate—who she hated anyway—was out, so it was just the two of us.

When I arrived, Sam was blustering about her room, getting ready. She was in a form-fitting dress that barely covered her rear. Her short, blonde hair was styled in that wild, sexy way the guys all seemed to love. With one hand holding her spiked black high-heeled shoe, she was digging around the clothes all over the floor trying to find the other one. She seemed particularly agitated. Sam's got a fiery personality anyway, but we'd been friends long enough that I sensed something else was going on.

"What's wrong?" I asked. I was standing in the middle of the room, not wanting to sit on her roommate's bed, even though I was right next to it, and not wanting to brave the mountain of clothes to cross to Sam's bed either. We were leaving in a couple minutes anyway.

"Oh..." Sam hedged, still digging. Maybe she was too upset to talk about whatever it was. She unearthed the missing heel and plopped down on her bed in a huff. "I'm just a little freaked out." She started to put on one shoe. "I'm three fucking days late on my period. Apparently fucking Harry doesn't know how to put a condom on because it broke on us a couple weeks ago."

I couldn't even remember which guy Harry was, Sam rotated through them so quickly. I was overtaken with fear for her, but my own history came back in a rush too. A buzzing sensation crawled over my skin and I slowly sank to her roommate's bed.

"I think I need to go get a goddamned pregnancy test." Heels finally on her feet, Sam huffed in frustration and stood. "All right, let's go."

I blinked at her, trying to keep my wits about me. "Are you sure you want to? Are you okay? We could go get a test right now if you want."

Sam sighed, considering. "I don't know. I don't know if I'm ready to deal with it if I am. But it's been kind of haunting me all day."

"Come on." I stood. "Let's get you one, and then you'll know."

So we did, and as we went to the store for the test, and later as she went to the bathroom to take it, I tried not to let my memories of doing all those things the year before haunt me. I tried not to start aching over Erik again, something I still did often even though I really didn't want to. What kept it all at bay was my worry for Sam. I didn't want her going through all that.

If she came out of that bathroom with a look of dread on her face, I was prepared to give her my support.

What I wasn't prepared for was what actually happened.

She came out triumphant, arms up, big grin on her face. "Halle-fucking-lujah!"

Relief on her behalf washed over me and I jumped up, smiling too. I gave her a big congratulatory hug.

"Maybe I'll try those birth control shots after all. The pill doesn't agree with me but I don't think I want to bank on condoms anymore."

That was the instant I went from smiling and celebrating with her, to completely breaking down. A dam somewhere deep inside me burst and knocked the shit out of me before sweeping me downstream.

"Hey." Sam furrowed her brows at what she must have thought were tears of relief, but still had a half grin on her face. "I think you were more worried about me than I was."

My tears escalated to sobbing and I sank to the bed, covering my face. Sam sat next to me, her arm on my back. "What the hell?" she said softly. "Honey, what's wrong?"

It all came out then. I hadn't told anyone else on the planet my story. My parents knew and that was it. But I told Sam everything. Absolutely everything, including how much I was still hurting about it and how nothing I did seemed to help.

Who knew it would take wild, little Sam to help me through it? She listened and commiserated with me. When I talked about how I'd been with boys she grew even more concerned.

"Listen," she said firmly, "You need to step back from men for a while."

I blinked at her in disbelief. I couldn't have been more surprised if she'd said she found sex to be an absolute bore. "Huh?"

"It's not good for you. God, you're like a lost little girl right now. Fucking a bunch of guys is only going to make that worse."

I still didn't know what to say. I couldn't believe Sam was saying this, but yet, what she was saying felt right. In fact, hearing those words out of her mouth felt like such a relief.

I gave her a quizzical look. "Not the Samantha Lawson advice I would have expected."

She shrugged easily. "Look, I know people judge me for the way I am with boys, but I don't really give a shit. It's not hurting the guys I'm with and it's not hurting <u>me.</u> I know what I'm doing. It's <u>fun.</u> That's it. I don't want anything more than that and I look for guys who feel the same way, because I'm not interested in screwing around with some dude's heart. But this is not fun for you. It's destructive and making you completely miserable. You need a better way to cope, sweetie."

I nodded slightly in agreement. "It used to be my music. Erik kind of..." I paused, trying to find the right words. "It's like he's all wrapped up in it now, and I don't want him to be. I... I miss how it used to be with the music. It used to be mine."

"Fuck that shit. It's still yours. Your music belonged to you before he ever came into the picture. Don't let him take it from you now. When you sit down at that piano, you find a way to make it yours again."

181

It took some time, but eventually, I did just that.

I took Sam's advice and stepped back from boys, and I kept the drinking under control. Sam was a big help there too, because even though she had a high tolerance for alcohol and could really put it away, I'd never once seen her really drunk.

I realized I'd been holding back with my music, and bumped my practicing hours up to where they should have been all along. I put in extra time after practicing my assigned pieces and—this was probably the biggest thing—I started to play around with the music I heard in my head.

I hadn't improvised at all since Erik and I had done it together, but since the music in my head was just mine, playing it made the piano just mine again too. Whatever part of me had been huddled and hiding from the music let go, and I started making better progress in the program.

I never did tell Chloe and Isabella my story. It wasn't because I couldn't. I knew I could tell them and they'd accept and support me just like Sam did. Maybe that's exactly what made me feel like I didn't need to say anything. It didn't feel like I was hiding a dark secret. I simply didn't tell them because talking to Sam unlocked something inside me, and I didn't want to curse it. I was finally starting to get better and leave things in my past at last. Why mess with what was working?

After a time, I dated a bit. Eventually I figured it was time to move on, even though part of me would always have a soft spot for my first love.

That's how it works for everybody, right?

There have been a few guys I've gotten deep in enough to be intimate with, but they've all fizzled out in the end. They never got that high off the ground to start with, in spite of them being good guys. But I'm okay with not having a serious relationship. My chosen career path isn't exactly friendly to that kind of thing anyway, what with all the traveling concert pianists have to do. The toll on relationships is famous in my field. But I don't need it. My music has taken over my soul in the big way it used to.

I've often thought there may not be room enough in my heart to love a man the way I know I can <u>and</u> love my music the way I do.

Then Erik shows up at that pre-audition for the competition, over five years after the last time I saw him, and it all comes back to me.

It was all in the past. Over. Sure, my heart still hurt if I thought about him too much, but the easy fix to that was just not to think about him too much. Everyone kind of aches for their first love from time to time anyway, don't they? You can't let stuff like that stop you from being happy.

And I haven't. I've been happy. I have.

But now he's here, on my turf, and I'm trapped.

Now <u>I'm</u> the one who wants to run.

The Here and Now

Chapter 11

I'm in the living room at Sam's house, a little fixer-upper she bought a few months ago only a mile from Hartman College and a couple miles from her job where she works as a graphic designer. The house has a distinct seventies feel, but she has a fun vision for it. Until she gets around to actually making changes, though, the walls will remain what Sam refers to as "puke" green. Sam and I are sitting cross-legged on the pink shag carpet and video chatting with Chloe and Isabella.

Chloe's just an hour and a half away, on the coast in Swan Pointe. She and her boyfriend Grayson live there, but they come up from time to time to hang out with us. Isabella, on the other hand, is in her second year of grad school—like me—and is clear across the country at Harvard working on her masters in microbiology.

The four of us Firework Girls group text pretty regularly, but when I started telling them about a certain ghost from my past named Erik, it was easier to get Chloe and Isabella caught up on screen. Now that my past has reappeared in my present, I'm going to need all the support from my friends I can get. I wish I'd waited for Jack to get here too, because telling the story has worn me out and I don't want to have to do it all over again.

"Wow..." Isabella says, once I've finished and we're all sitting in silence, taking it all in. Isabella trails off, like she's not sure what to say. I'm fidgeting with my hair, which I've only worn in a single braid for years now. Hell, I don't know what to say either.

She leans heavily back in her chair. She's sitting at her desk, I can tell. Her long, brown hair is pulled up into a bun and she has a pencil stuck in it. There's an impressive stack of massive textbooks off to one side.

She sighs, crosses her copper-colored arms, and tilts her head, considering me. "So where are you with him?"

"Nowhere," I say firmly. "I don't want to be anywhere with him. I don't want to talk to him. I don't want to see him. I don't want him anywhere near me." I groan in frustration and toss my braid behind me. "I can't believe he's here!"

"Did he transfer here or something?" Chloe asks. She's lying on her stomach on her bed, her auburn hair tucked around in front of one shoulder and her feet kicking up behind her. Even on screen, her ice-blue eyes are striking. "He definitely wasn't there last year right?"

I shake my head.

"Maybe he transferred here from somewhere else because he knew you'd be here," Sam says next to me.

"I don't know. If anything, he probably thought I wouldn't be. Even if he assumed I came here for my undergrad degree, he probably thought I'd be gone by now. Most people go somewhere different for their graduate work."

"Why didn't you?" Sam asks, cocking her head at me.

"Hartman has a great program." That was mostly the reason. I don't need to add that I was scared to apply anywhere else. I barely admit that one to myself.

"Didn't you say he looked shocked to see you?" Isabella asks, returning to the topic at hand.

I nod, reliving that moment when Erik met my eyes. He looked as mortified to see me as I'd felt about seeing him. I still feel the echoes of what it was like to pass him in the aisle, my body tuned into him like a beacon.

Then I remember what happened next, how I fumbled over my own fingers like I'd never played the piano before in my life. Sure, I pulled it around in the end, but I wasn't happy with my performance, and clearly Professor Reinecht wasn't either.

Erik, on the other hand, played like a god.

"Ugh. I can't believe he's in the competition. I'm so screwed."

"Oh, come on," Isabella says, reassuringly, leaning forward in her chair. "You're always nervous about this stuff."

"And you never have any reason to be," Chloe adds, kicking her feet slightly behind her.

I know what they're talking about. If I'm forced to be honest with myself, I know I don't have as much faith in my abilities as maybe I should. Sometimes I still can't believe how far I've come as a musician. It doesn't seem like a girl like me should have the kind of success I've had. That self-doubt is a recurring theme I can't seem to shake. This would not be the first time my girls have had to give me encouragement before a competition or performance.

But this is different. This is Erik.

"You don't understand," I say soberly. "His music is like something from another planet. I can't beat that. I know I can't."

Sam huffs next to me. "Well, not if you think like that you won't. No one's unbeatable. Especially when they're playing against you, girl."

Isabella and Chloe both nod in agreement. I don't argue. I guess we'll find out soon enough.

"Thanks for your support," I say glumly.

"Give it your best," Isabella says.

I nod. I will. It probably won't matter in the end, but I will.

"I still want to know what he's doing here," Sam says sternly. She sounds like she's ready to hunt Erik down and hogtie him somewhere as punishment for hurting her friend. Knowing Sam, she's probably thinking something along those lines. It'll only get worse when Jack's in the mix. They've been known for taking matters into their own hands before. After all, they were the ones to come up with the prank that earned us our name, the Firework Girls.

Of course, that was our freshman year in college. We've all grown up a lot since then. Sam and Jack are getting too old for those kinds of shenanigans.

I glance at the mischievous look on Sam's face.

At least, I think they are.

"Are you sure you don't want to talk to him?" Chloe asks. "Even if only to find out what happened?"

191

"I know what happened," I say firmly. "He abandoned me. I don't give a shit why he did it."

By the time I'm in my one-on-one session with Professor Reinecht the next day, I'm feeling a little better. After talking to my girls (and later Jack, when he showed up for a late-night raid on Sam's pantry), I feel like I have a kind of armor around me. I'm not here alone. I have my friends. And like Jack said, Hartman belongs to me more than it does to Erik. "Let him avoid you," Jack had said.

That part is easier said than done, it turns out. I have been glancing around for Erik everywhere I go, especially in the music building. But I haven't seen him. I've had at least one session of all my classes this semester, so I know we don't share any, thank God. But lately I haven't gone to the Gizmo—the college's on-campus cafe I tend to haunt—and I took a different walking route this morning. I usually walk along the outskirts of campus, but didn't want to risk seeing him.

In session, I can tell Professor Reinecht is a little miffed about my screw up on stage yesterday. "What happened with your audition, Ashley? That was pathetic."

"Sorry," I say, my cheeks flushing a bit. "It was something personal. I won't let it happen again."

He grunts and taps the sheet music for my competition piece, indicating the conversation is over and he wants me to play. I'm getting off easy. He's a notoriously tough task-master. Some students complain about it, but given how brutal the music world is, he'd be doing no one any favors by treating us with kid gloves. I like that he's blunt, because then when he praises me I know I'm really doing something right.

As I begin to play, he paces next to the piano with gusto, another habit students find annoying. Several measures in, he gives a sharp, "Ah!"

I stop obediently.

"Listen." He taps his ear. He plays the left-hand only of two bars. "This. Not this." He plays it again, and I can hear the difference. "Understand?"

I nod. Professor Reinecht is a man of few words. He's told me before he likes that I can <u>hear</u> his instruction without him having to waste a bunch of words on it. He's unlike any professor at Hartman, that's for sure, but he's my favorite. He retired from his own successful career after playing in celebrated halls all over the world and he's brilliant. He was one of the reasons I wanted to continue my graduate degree at Hartman.

"Again." He resumes his pacing.

I start over. When I get through the measure he just corrected he keeps pacing instead of stopping me, a good sign. We continue on this way until we've gone all the way through the number together.

He stops by the piano. "How are your practice sessions?"

I give him a rundown of my current routine and he nods with approval. "Double your time on this." He taps the sheet music in front of me.

"Okay."

"See you next week."

I get up and gather the music together. "Do you think I'll do all right in the competition?" I try not to sound nervous.

He nods, and I feel heartened. I expect him to say something encouraging. I can count on him for that almost as much as I can count on my Firework Girls. But what he says is this: "It'll be a tough run this year."

Feeling somewhat deflated, I pack my bag. I don't want to ask why he thinks it'll be a tough run.

I'd rather not hear him say it aloud.

After a few more days go by without running into Erik, I start to relax a bit. Whatever his schedule is, it doesn't seem to overlap with mine. The fact that he's at Hartman at all almost starts to fade into the background. The only time I really think about it is when I'm practicing for the competition, which I've been doing with gusto.

I added the Gizmo back into my routine yesterday, but today is the day I regret it. As I pick up my caramel macchiato from the barista, I turn to find Erik right behind me. I stop cold. He's looking right at me, and God, he's so close. Not invading-my-personal-space close, but yet again my body seems so in tune with his physical location, I feel like a moth being pulled to the flame.

I hold my ground though. He burned me once. That was more than enough.

"Hi Ashley," he says quietly. "I've been looking for you."

I frown at him. "Really? I've been avoiding you."

He nods, contrite. Or he appears that way anyway. Who the hell knows what he's really thinking? "Do you think we could talk?"

Oh now he wants to talk? Fuck that. I walk around him and head for the door. "Leave me alone."

I leave the Gizmo and cross the patio to the campus grounds. He doesn't follow me.

I'm disappointed that he doesn't follow me.

I hate us both for that.

I don't see him again until the competition that Friday. When they sent out the schedules, I knew I was bound to see him. They've grouped the pianists together and he plays immediately after I do. <u>Of course.</u>

There's a lot of milling around the backstage of Kopp Hall. This competition doesn't quite call for the formal gowns of many of the performances I've done, but nice dress is still required. I'm wearing a sapphire gown with a form-fitting bodice and calf-length flowing skirt. As I do for any public performance, I've taken the time to style my hair so it's flowing to my waist in gentle curls.

We first see one another from a distance. Or rather, this is the moment I first see him. Judging by the way he's taking me in, I gather he noticed me a few moments before. He has a stunned, appreciative look on his face. I'm flattered in spite of myself, but that only makes me more frustrated. That fact that he looks so scrumptious in his suit coat and red tie is not helping matters.

His eyes meet mine. I look away. I head for the little table in the wings and check in with the assistant sitting there. She takes my name and gives me a number to hold up for the judges when I go on stage.

With this little bit of business done, I busy myself checking the program. A fellow second-year grad student is on stage, someone I've noticed has really improved since he's been in the program. There are still four more players to get through before it's my turn, and I can feel Erik <u>right over there.</u>

I glance at him. Our eyes meet for the briefest second before he looks away, like he's been caught.

God, this is torture. My heart is racing, partly because I'm feeling trapped with nowhere to go and partly because he's so damned handsome. Why is my body responding to him still? After all this time and after everything?

I'm an idiot.

I find a place to wait, as far away from him as I can reasonably get, and try to focus on why I'm here. Determinedly ignoring the pounding of my heart, I close my eyes and start to go through my pre-performance routine: deep breaths, mentally running through the piece, finger stretches.

I glance at him again. He's sitting in a chair, legs outstretched, arms crossed, head slightly down. He looks sad, and like he's a million miles away.

I soften slightly. An old impulse in me wants to go over and comfort him. But I don't. We aren't who we were all those years ago. And if he feels badly, he deserves it.

The performer before me finally takes his place at the piano.

As he begins his piece, I move closer so I can wait just off stage. Since I don't have the end of my braid to play with, I keep running my thumb over the corner of my number placard.

As the performer before me finishes up and bows to the judges, I hear the footfalls of someone approaching from behind. By the way my skin is on alert, I know it has to be him. He settles to my right, waiting.

I look over at him. He's looking at me too.

Why? I want to ask him. Why did you leave me like that?

Our eyes hold for a moment. The prior pianist leaves the stage, passing by us. My name is called. "Good luck," Erik says softly.

I don't answer. I don't know if he's trying to trip me up or not, but I'm not going to have a repeat of last time. I hold up my number for the judges, sit at the bench, and do my best to forget everything while playing Beethoven's sonata.

At the conclusion I stand, hold my number again, and wait.

The judges call out my score—the highest pianist yet, I note—and dismiss me from the stage. My body hums as I draw closer to him. He's waiting in the wings. I don't look at him and I don't wish him luck. I head straight back to the little table and turn in my number.

Then my old friend, the Pied Piper, begins to play.

I hover at the table, listening.

Slowly, I'm drawn closer to the stage, against my will. He is magic. His music ambrosia. I want to consume it.

I won't get the judges' comments until tomorrow, but if I were to describe my own performance, I would use words that have often been used to describe me in the past: "Flawless. Technically strong. A beautiful delivery."

With a resigned sort of detachment, I know what I did and can call it as it was, without all the self-doubt that tends to hover over me like a black cloud. The fact that I did well doesn't really matter though. Because if I were a judge describing Erik's piece, I would say: "Stunning. Bold. Confident."

He's beyond technically proficient, and I already know I've been beat. If the judges don't score him higher than me, they're morons.

The next pianist on the program comes up next to me. "Pretty fucking good for a first year grad student," she says, envy dripping off her every word.

"A first year grad?" I turn to her. Erik should be in his second year, like me. "Are you sure?"

She nods and we both listen as Erik receives his score.

A full twenty points above my own.

Chapter 12

Even though I'm in our favorite bar on Eighth street with Sam and Jack, I'm in a dark place. I don't think it's just because of the competition today either, but I'm not prepared to fully admit that to myself.

Jack has one lanky arm thrown around my shoulder, in an attempt to comfort me. Like Sam, Jack's hair has a mind of its own, but it works for him. He's got that shaggy Benedict Cumberbatch look going on that the girls love.

"He doesn't belong here," I say. "I don't even know what he's doing at rinky dink Hartman. He has his degree from fucking Juilliard."

"Hartman isn't rinky dink," Sam says, calmly. "You've said yourself they have one of the best music programs in the country."

"Everybody's rinky dink compared to Juilliard."

"You're just being ridiculous and bitter." Leave it to Sam to call it like she sees it. She's probably right.

"Hey, hey," Jack says somewhat jovially and squeezing my shoulders. He's clearly trying to lighten my mood. I have to admit, it's past time. I've sulked plenty. "It's okay if Ashley wants to be ridiculous and bitter. That's why we're where the booze is."

I crack half a smile. "We're here so you can pick up on girls."

He gives me a mock, insulted look and puts his hand to his chest. "I'm offended!" Sam and I exchange looks and she rolls her eyes amusedly.

"Uh-huh," she says.

"I didn't come here to pick up on girls."

I look at him, waiting for it.

"These girls are here to pick up on me."

"There it is," Sam says smiling and I can't help but smile too. Jack grins at me, satisfied.

I take a deep breath, trying to get myself under control. It's been a long time since I haven't placed first in a competition. Maybe

I'm just not used to it and feeling a little raw. Maybe I'll feel better tomorrow.

God, I hope so.

Giving a resolute sigh, I lean against Jack and look at Sam. She smiles at me knowingly and I shrug. "What am I going to do?"

"You're going to drink another beer." She raises my nearly empty bottle to get the attention of the waiter.

I take the bottle from her and drink down the rest. Sam's right. For the moment anyway, that's about all I can do.

The following Tuesday I head to the Gizmo for the first time since I saw Erik there before. It's my favorite place for coffee, and I'm tired of avoiding it. I've resigned myself to the fact that I'm going to see Erik plenty of times between now and the end of the year. It probably won't be the last time he kicks my ass in a competition either. I may as well try to get used to it.

I go three whole times before running into him again. Just as I was starting to get relaxed about being here, I see him waiting at the end of the line at the counter, right as I'm coming in. I briefly consider leaving, but instead I sigh resolutely and come up behind him. I'm a big girl. I can handle this.

I do give myself twice the normal amount of space between us though.

He noticed me when I was coming through the door. At first it seemed like he wasn't going to try to talk to me either, but after we shuffle forward in line one place, he slowly turns. "Hey," he says quietly.

I pause. I guess I can be civil. "Hi."

"How's it going?"

I frown at him. <u>How's it going?</u>

He sighs at himself. "Sorry."

I shrug. Whatever. "It's fine."

We shuffle forward again.

"Listen..." he says hesitantly, "Could I... buy you a coffee or something?"

I consider saying something smartass about how I can afford my own coffee, but I know that's not what he means. He wants to talk. Really talk. I don't know if I want to.

I don't know if I can.

But there's that part of me that wants to know, what in the hell happened all those years ago?

We scoot forward. There's only one person in front of him now. It's a young undergrad, from the looks of it. She's hemming and hawing over the gluten-free baked goods in the display case.

"Please?" Erik asks.

I'm considering giving in, but I'm not ready to commit. Instead I ask a different question that's been on my mind. "Is it true you're only a first year grad student?"

He looks a bit taken aback. He almost seems pained. This lasts only for a split second. He nods. "I took a year off."

"Why?"

His hesitation—and pain—is more obvious now. We're suddenly pulled into the kind of intimate moment we used to share. My heart softens in spite of myself. Before I have a chance to resist it, he says, "My parents were in a car accident about a month after I graduated from Juilliard. It killed my dad instantly." My hand flies to my mouth.

"My mom's okay now, mostly, but she was messed up pretty badly. She was in the hospital for six weeks and intensive rehab for several months. She's still in rehab, but just once a week now."

"God," I say stupidly, having to resist the urge to put my hand on his arm. "I'm so sorry."

He nods slightly in acknowledgement of this. "Is your tomato soup gluten free?" the girl at the counter asks. Erik and I look at each other awkwardly for a moment. "How are you doing?" I finally ask.

He sighs. "I'd really be better if you'd let me get you a coffee."

We sit at a table in the back corner and sip our coffees in uncomfortable silence. I'm not sure how to begin the conversation. Maybe Erik isn't either.

Finally, he sets down his cup, leans in slightly on both elbows, and looks me in the eye. "I know it's a little late for this, but I owe you an apology."

An unexpected lump forms in my throat but I swallow it down.

"I know it can't make up for everything that happened. I can't even imagine what you went through and—" he stops abruptly. He looks down, blinking at the table, apparently suppressing some unexpected emotion of his own.

I try not to let myself be swayed by it. I really do.

He takes a determined sip of his coffee, then looks at me again. I'm captured by his eyes. Maybe I'm a fool, but all I see in him is sincerity and pain and regret.

"I know there's no fixing it. I'm not trying to do that. I just thought you deserved to hear me tell you how terribly, <u>terribly</u>"—and here his voice cracks—"sorry I am. You didn't deserve any of that."

The lump in my throat has made a reappearance, but I still refuse to cry. "You promised me I wouldn't go through that alone."

He nods and closes his eyes briefly. "I know. I didn't want you to be alone."

"Then why was I?" I say earnestly. I realize I said that louder than intended, but I don't bother looking around. I lower my voice and lean in, still holding his eyes. "Why didn't you come to me? Call me? Something."

He looks down and frowns at his cup. He digs his thumbnail into the cardboard at the base. "I don't want to give you excuses," he says at last.

I sit back and sigh. "Well, that's fine for you, but I'd sure as hell like an explanation."

His eyes fly up to mine. I'm still frowning at him and he seems to be taking me in, like it had never occurred to him that I might just want answers.

"Okay." He takes a deep breath, then says again, "Okay."

I slowly cross my arms, not as a sign of anger, but just because it feels safer. Right now it's the only defense I have.

"After I left your house that night," he says slowly, our eyes watching each other hesitantly, "I went home and told my mom what was going on. She..." He stops and frowns at the cup again. He takes a deep breath, then looks at me resolutely.

"She said the easiest thing would be for you to get an abortion. When I told her that's not what was going to happen, she panicked and got my dad involved. I told him I loved you and planned to see things through. He said he'd talk to your folks and work things out, but I didn't understand what he meant by that until he got back and told me what he'd done. Once I realized what was really going on, I kind of kicked myself for thinking he was on my side. Looking back I think he didn't show his cards right away for a reason." Erik shakes his head a bit and shrugs. "My dad was a lawyer, remember."

"Yeah," I say dully. "I remember."

Erik clenches his jaw. "Well, yeah. That's the thing isn't it? That's why he acted so fast. He had to make sure he had everything in motion so I couldn't fight him on it."

Erik leans forward more, his face getting earnest. "I did try at first, Ashley. I really did. I fought my dad so hard about it that night, they confiscated my phone so I couldn't contact you. I didn't say what my plans were. I was trying to play my cards close to the vest too, but I think my dad, at least, knew they had to get me out of there because if they went to sleep that night, they'd wake up to find me gone in the morning. And you know what?" His eyes get a look of hard determination. "No way was I going to stay with them any longer than I had to. I planned to get the hell out and come to you the second their back was turned."

He looks down at the table, breathing hard. He's gripping his cup with both hands now.

So what happened? I want to know, but it's all I can do to keep my own emotions under control. If I say a word, the lump in my throat will take over. I can't let that happen. I won't cry. I refuse.

I watch him as he takes a steadying breath. The muscles in his face are flexing as he clenches his jaw.

"They called the airline to get last minute flights to New York and the next thing I know, my mom's packing my bags. My dad and I nearly came to blows because at first I refused to leave the house." His eyes are fixed rigidly on his cup. " That's when my dad made it perfectly clear his talk of prosecuting you was serious business. He was more than willing to destroy you and your family and ruin your life. He <u>wanted</u> to. The only reason he didn't is because—" His voice breaks again, but he takes a hard breath and continues firmly, "because he knew that leverage was the only thing keeping me at bay. And he was right. It did keep me at bay."

Erik pinches his eyes shut, then looks at me earnestly.

I swallow hard against the lump in my throat. I can't. I can't cry with him.

"I backed down," he says softly. "I just... didn't know how to protect you from him. The longer things went on, and I thought about what you had to be going through... I knew you had to hate me. And who could blame you?"

He takes a steadying breath and leans back in his chair. "My dad said I lost the privilege of graduating from the Academy.

He pulled some strings and got me into a private high school in the city. I finished things out there. By the time they gave me a new phone, it didn't matter anymore. I knew they would do anything they could to keep me away from you. I wasn't going to risk him throwing you in jail."

We sit there in silence. He's frowning and staring at the table like he's somewhere else.

I can only look at him and try not to cry for both of us. I feel a twinge of guilt for hating a dead man, but it's how I feel anyway. I wish I could go back in time and know what Erik was going through. But I can't. And while there's part of me that feels a sort of... understanding at least, it doesn't change the fact that our relationship was shattered beyond repair a long time ago.

"Ashley," Erik says softly, "I'm really not trying to give you excuses."

I nod, still unable to risk speaking. My hands are clenched together on my lap. My entire body is clenched. It's like if I move at all, the dam will burst.

"And I'm not trying to..." he takes another deep breath. "I know it's too late for us. I just... I just thought you deserved to hear..." He holds my eyes.

God, there he is, the boy I loved so long ago.

"I'm so, so sorry."

The tears are building in my eyes now, I can't stop them, so I look down at the hands in my lap and nod. I nod again.

<u>Okay,</u> I think. <u>Okay, I hear you.</u> But I can't talk.

Slowly but determinedly, I get to my feet.

I brush my fingertips on the top of his hand, the only acknowledgment I can give him, and hurry away.

Chapter 13

I somehow make it to my beat-up old hatchback but cry all the way to Sam's house. She's not even home from work yet, so of course Jack isn't there either. He works from home as a web designer, but practically lives here in his off hours, like I do. Why Sam is the hub of our lives, I don't know for sure, but she is.

I put on a light movie to cheer myself up—<u>Pitch Perfect</u>—but manage to frown at the screen and leak tears onto the pillow on Sam's couch the whole way through.

Then, as if I didn't have enough to process, I get an email that was sent out to all music majors, announcing an upcoming national competition, the Myra Hess Piano Competition. There are going to be three rounds. Each school will hold their own round and send two musicians in each category to one of four regional competitions. The kicker? The top three from each region will compete in the finals at Lincoln Center in New York City.

God, Lincoln Center.

I toss my phone on the pink shag carpet. I can't hardly think about another competition right now. My mind's still too busy running over everything that happened when we were teens, looking at it again with fresh eyes. Erik hadn't been ignoring my texts and phone calls, his parents took his phone and then got him a different one. He didn't run from me, he was practically taken. Threatened.

I remember how frightened I'd been by his father's threats, and wonder how I would have handled it if I didn't have my parents to support me. Erik was still just a kid and didn't have anyone. He didn't even have me.

When Sam gets home, I tell her the whole story and, later, listen with a sort of numbness as she relays everything to Jack. I'm too drained to do it myself. I'm lying on my stomach on the couch and Jack is kneeling next to me, rubbing my back in slow, firm motions.

One of my arms is hanging off the couch. Sam is sitting on the floor, holding my hand, and rubbing my arm.

"Do you want to watch a movie or something?" she suggests. I've already turned down Sam's suggestion of ice cream, and Jack's of hard liquor.

But I don't answer. I've finally found a way to voice the thing I've been afraid of since Erik first told me his side of things. "Do you guys think I'd be weak," I say slowly, "if I forgave him?"

Sam exchanges a glance with Jack before looking back at me. "You mean, so you can get back together with him?"

I shake my head once. "No. It's too late for that," I say, echoing what Erik said earlier. He's probably right. "I just... I kind of feel like I forgive him. Does that make me foolish?"

"No, honey," Sam says.

"It doesn't?"

Sam sighs. "It sounds like he was just as much a victim of his dad as the rest of you were. Don't you think?" she asks, looking up at Jack.

There's a bit of a pause as Jack continues to rub the aches out of my shoulders. "Yes," he says at last. "Part of me wants to say he needed to man up but, that's probably me just feeling protective of you. He was only a kid, like you were. And what <u>would</u> have happened if his dad had pressed charges against you?" Jack rubs his thumbs firmly up either side of my spine. "Ya cradle robber," he says gently.

I crack a faint smile and Sam smiles back at me. I feel a little lighter, trying my new-found forgiveness on for size.

"So since we're not mad at him anymore," Jack says, sighing, "I guess trapping him inside of a piano case is out."

I don't even want to know if he's kidding.

"Though that would still be a way to get him out of the way for the competition," he says, like he's trying to tempt me.

"No thanks." I smile. I had mentioned the competition, but we didn't discuss it much. It's funny how even something that huge seems small in the face of everything else going on.

By the time we finally settle in to watch a movie—The Princess Bride, which we've all seen about a hundred times—I'm feeling strengthened. At peace almost.

Sam and I are both curled against Jack, whose long legs are draped across the coffee table. His arms are stretched along the back of the couch. Halfway through the movie, right before Princess Buttercup is about to push Wesley down the hill, Sam keeps her eyes on the screen and asks softly, "Do you still have feelings for him?"

I don't answer right away. If I'm honest with myself, yes. There's a part of me that's always loved Erik, and probably always will. But I don't think that's what Sam is asking. Frankly, I think she already knows. I suspect she's asking about our future, or if I think we even have one.

But five years and that much hurt is an awfully big gap to bridge. It's been so long, I don't even know who he is anymore. He doesn't know me anymore either. I keep hearing the words he said earlier: "It's too late for us."

It's not until Wesley rescues Princess Buttercup from the lightning sand, and she's hanging onto him and saying, "We'll never succeed," that I finally respond to Sam.

"I just... don't want to be mad at him anymore."

"Hmm."

"Then don't be," Jack says, rubbing my shoulder reassuringly before putting his arm back on the couch.

"Meanwhile, kicking his ass in the competition might help a little bit in the revenge department," Sam says.

I smile. "I don't want revenge."

She raises her head slightly to look at me. Her short blonde hair is always sticking out in different directions, but one side is extra wonky since she's been lying against Jack's chest. "But you wouldn't mind kicking his ass in the competition right?"

"Sam, I want to kick everyone's ass in the competition. That has nothing to do with him."

She puts her head back down, satisfied. "Well then, you go do that."

"Just like Wesley is kicking the ass out of that Rodent of Unusual Size," Jack says.

But I don't know if I can.

Letting go of my anger seems like a far easier task than outplaying Erik Williams.

In the weeks leading up to the school rounds of the Myra Hess Competition, Erik and I haven't done more than say hello when we see each other at the Gizmo. We've given each other a few tentative smiles, though, and every time, my heart feels a kind of release. I hadn't realized how hard it was on me, to be mad at him all this time.

I don't miss that anger.

I try not to think about whether or not I miss him.

Meanwhile, I'm trying to focus on my life as it is now: classes, friends, and practicing the hell out of my competition piece.

In spite of my best efforts, I was right about one thing. It's been far easier to forgive Erik than it was to outplay him. I did my best, but at the end of the school rounds, my heart sinks when they call my name for second place.

I put a gracious smile on my face anyway, and kind of shrug at my group of cheerleaders in the audience: Sam, Jack, and even Chloe and Grayson, who drove up from Swan Pointe just for the occasion. They're smiling back at me and clapping enthusiastically.

I keep my smile in place while they announce the winner and I watch him walk up to the stage. I console myself that at least I get to move on to regionals. The competition isn't over yet.

In theory, anyway.

As he comes up next to me, I feel a confusing mix of resentment and pride.

His piece was truly magnificent. I wish someone would have recorded it and put it on iTunes as if we were American Idol contestants, then I could buy it and listen to him play over and over again.

Just like I used to do.

As we leave the stage and go into the wings, I give him a sincere, "Congratulations."

"You too," he says, though he's giving me an apologetic look. "Sorry."

I sigh. He understands what's going on here as well as I do. But what else is new? Erik's always been better than me. "Why are you sorry?" He really shouldn't have to be sorry about placing first in a competition.

He sighs. "I'm sorry for a lot of things."

I nod and look away. "I know you are. It's okay."

And just like someone flipped a switch in me, I've done all I can handle. I'm not mad, I just need a breath.

"I'll see you around." I give him a small wave and head for my bag.

He lets me go and this time, I'm glad. But I feel better, like I've taken a step toward something, though I'm not sure what.

Chapter 14

In lieu of our traditional post-performance tradition of Volcano fries at Delsa's Diner, I opt for Rounders, the bar on Eighth Street. I'm actually surprised at how well I'm dealing with this latest blow to my ego, but a drink sure isn't going to hurt anything.

The five of us are sitting around a table far enough away from the DJ and the dance floor that we're able to talk. Chloe's on her phone, texting Isabella in Boston. We've all been trying to reschedule our upcoming group trip to the Rivers Paradise Resort in Swan Pointe, this one including the guys, since the next round of competition interferes with our original plans.

Finding new dates that work for everyone has been a challenge. Chloe and Grayson have been the hardest ones to work around, since they travel so much for the website they launched together several months ago. It's called "A Guy and A Girl Take on the World" and uses both their website and their YouTube channel to cover travel, adventure, and food. They're pretty entertaining together, actually, and have already amassed quite the following.

It's been easier, since most of us are all here together, to look at the calendar and find a weekend that we hope works for the trip. Chloe's just checking to see if Isabella's available. Grayson's sitting next to her, his arm draped on the back of her chair. He's absently playing with a lock of Chloe's auburn hair.

Meanwhile, Sam has returned to the topic of this evening's competition. "I gotta say, you didn't mention how cute Erik is. I mean, he's a fucking hottie, isn't he?"

"You said it," Chloe agrees, still typing in the message on her phone.

"Hey!" Grayson says, pretending to be offended.

Chloe looks at him and smiles. "But not as hot as you, baby."

I'm not sure I agree with Chloe's assessment of who's hotter, but I don't say so. It's irrelevant anyway.

Chloe gives him a kiss and he settles back in his chair, satisfied. I smile. I think he was just fishing for a kiss to start with. "Okay, those dates work for her." Chloe puts down her phone. "We're all set."

"Perfect." Sam nudges Jack with her elbow. "Now we just have to find dates." The talent these two have for plucking dates out of thin air astonishes me.

"Thanks for changing things," I say again.

"Of course." Sam waves her hand dismissively. "You can't miss your chance to hand Erik's ass to him."

"Right." I nod and try to look confident. It's partially for my own benefit and partially to keep Sam satisfied. If she thinks I'm doubting myself, she'll harp on it and I'd rather just move on to another topic of conversation.

The DJ starts to play "Thinking Out Loud" and Chloe and Grayson immediately look at one another, smiling. "That's our song!" Chloe says.

227

"Come on, sweetheart," he says, and leads her to the dance floor.

"They're so freaking cute together," Sam says easily, taking a drink. I'm proud of how little it bothers her to see Chloe and Grayson as a couple, considering how she'd once been caught up in the crossfires of that relationship.

Jack brings his glass up to his mouth, but before he takes a sip, he casually says to Sam, "There's a guy checking you out at nine o'clock."

Sam smiles at this bit of intelligence from her favorite wingman and subtly glances over. She and the intended target make eye contact. She gives him a subtle smile intended to lure him over.

I can already see it's going to work. Sure enough, he slides off his bar stool and heads over.

Sam grins. "Good work, Jack."

"You're welcome," he says, clearly pleased with himself. Within three minutes, Sam's been lured away and Jack and I are left to our own devices.

"What about you?" I ask. "Any prospects out there?"

"Eh." He shrugs. "I haven't really scoped the place out yet."

"Good," I say lightly. "You have to stay and make me feel like a desirable woman."

He frowns at me. "You <u>are</u> a desirable woman." I was just teasing, so I'm a little surprised by his serious reaction.

I pat his knee reassuringly. "Thanks, babe."

Jack gets a thoughtful look on his face.

"I was just kidding," I say, wondering what it was that got him so concerned. I'm not prepared for the next thing he says.

"Do you think my relationship with you girls is weird?"

"Weird?" I tilt my head at him. "Why would it be weird?"

"I don't know. Because of the way I am with you. All of you."

"You mean like our wild, screaming orgies?"

"Ashley!"

I laugh. I don't shock Jack too often, but when I do I get a special kind of pleasure from it.

"Damn, girl." He laughs and leans back in his chair. "Here I am trying to ask you a serious question."

He's joking, but not. I can see it in his eyes. I rub his arm.

"Sorry. I guess I know what you mean." For plutonic relationships, I realize we have a higher-than-normal level of physical contact with Jack. But it's just always been that way. I don't even remember how it started. Things have changed a bit in recent years though. "I notice you're different with Chloe and Isabella now."

"Isabella's married and Chloe may as well be," Jack says simply. "Grayson's not going anywhere."

I nod. There's no question about that.

His face is growing more and more serious though. Something about this is weighing on him. "Why are you asking, Jack?"

He only shrugs and takes a sip of his beer. "No reason, I guess."

I scoot a little closer and lean my chin on my hand. "Uh-huh."

He eyes me and sighs. He comes in closer, too. "Well, if I wanted to be in a relationship with a girl, would she think it's weird?"

I tilt my head at him. He seems genuinely concerned. "Do you have a girl in mind?"

"No. But it's bound to happen eventually, right?"

Yeah, it probably is. Now that I think about it, even though Jack isn't any more serious about girls than Sam is about boys, there've been far fewer of them than there used to be. Maybe our Jack is finally starting to grow up.

"Any girl who dates you should accept you for who you are. That includes how you are with your friends."

He nods, but still seems a little bothered.

"What's this really about, Jack?"

He shrugs again. "I don't know. I guess...." he pauses. "I guess I've been feeling a little unsettled lately. I see what Isabella and Chloe have and think maybe that'd be nice, but..."

231

"But what?"

He glances around a bit, stalling. Finally he says, "I don't know if I'm really boyfriend material, you know?"

"Ah Jack, are you kidding? You'd be an awesome boyfriend."

He looks at me a little desperately, like he really needs the reassurance. "I would?"

"Of course! You're one of the sweetest guys I know."

"Sweet?" He makes a face, like I've just insulted him, but I can tell he's not too bothered.

I laugh. "Yes, sweet. And fun and smart and so loyal. You'd do anything for your friends, right?"

"Well, yeah." He shrugs like it's no big deal.

"I can only imagine how you'd treat a girlfriend. You're so good to us, Jack. Any girl would be lucky to have you. Don't worry, the right girl for you is going to love you for who you are. I don't see you pairing up with the jealous type anyway. Any woman you fall for is going to be a strong woman, and a strong woman won't be threatened by your friends."

He gives me a smile. "Yeah, okay. Besides, how many guys know how to braid hair?" He gives the tail of my braid a little flick. "That's a plus in my corner, right?"

"You do it better than Chloe does," I say smiling. It's true, too.

He gives me a broad grin. "Damn right. I give killer back rubs, too."

"Yes, you do." I turn my back to him and bring my braid in front.

"Is that a hint?" he asks laughing.

I would tell him he still owes me my post-performance shoulder rub, but he's already squeezing my shoulders and making me melt right where I'm sitting.

We don't say any more, but it's not long before Jack's desire for a more meaningful relationship has me thinking.

About Erik.

By the time I see Professor Reinecht on Monday, I've recovered from the disappointment of the first round and am possessed with fresh determination to win the competition. After all, winners get to play at freaking <u>Lincoln Center</u>. I've been practicing my next piece like crazy all weekend, so I'm knocked a little off kilter when Professor Reinecht changes it.

"Are you sure?" I'm looking over the sheet music he's placed in front of me. "The other one is more demanding."

"Only by an inch. The mechanics of your playing is not the issue. Something in you flows when you play this one. That's what we want the judges to hear."

I don't argue over that. I know he's right.

We run through the piece once, and I ask him to go over it with me again before I'm left on my own for a couple of days. I want to make sure I'm practicing it the way he wants.

I skip lunch and go straight to the practice rooms, while his instructions are still fresh.

The next day, I head to the Gizmo after my morning class. This time when I spy Erik sipping his coffee at a back table by the window, I'm glad he's there.

I get my order, then walk up to him and wait until he looks up at me. His face registers surprise and maybe a little trepidation.

"You haven't offered to buy me coffee again," I say.

Erik starts to get up almost instantly, but freezes when he notices the cup I'm holding. "You already have coffee."

"I don't have a place to sit."

Giving a hesitant smile, he gestures to the chair opposite him. "Please."

I sit down and hang my bag on the back of the chair. He's giving me a questioning look. I smile and shrug. "I figured there's no reason we can't be friends and talk from time to time."

He smiles more broadly then. "I'm glad, Ashley."

It feels good to hear him say my name. I take a sip of my caramel macchiato.

"What do you want to talk about?"

"Well, I figure we have plenty of other stuff to catch up on. I haven't heard anything about your experience at Juilliard."

"You want to hear about that?"

"God yes," I say, and he laughs. "You know, I actually went to New York this summer with some friends and we saw Juilliard."

"You did? Did you go inside?"

"No. I just gazed at it from the back of Illumination Lawn."

He laughs. Something deep inside me I didn't know was still tense starts to uncoil. It's nice to talk to him and have it feel easy.

"So are you going to give me the dirt, or what?"

And that's how it begins. He tells me about Juilliard and how intense the competition is there. Things can get competitive here at Hartman, too, but he makes The Juilliard School sound like a whole different world. There's something underneath the way he talks about it that makes me wonder if he was happy there. From what he's saying, it sounds like he did well. Before I can ask more about it though, he insists I do some of the talking.

I steer away from the heavy stuff and tell him a bit about my experience with the program here.

"I'm so impressed with the way you're playing now," he interrupts to say.

I know I've improved, but sitting across from the man who could probably outplay me in his sleep makes my own accomplishments feel a little different. I change the subject and start telling him about my Firework Girls, and Jack.

"Jack sounds like a Firework Girl himself," Erik says, smiling.

"He's sort of the Firework Girl of Honor."

He checks his phone, which has been lying on the table. He told me about fifteen minutes ago he has a class soon. I get the feeling he's been pushing it, not wanting to leave.

I'm not quite ready for this to be over either, but I still ask, "When does class start?"

"I have one whole minute." He gives me a regretful look.

I smile. "You'd better get going."

"Yeah."

He sits there another few seconds though, and we just look at each other in silence, our eyes soft with understanding.

"This has been nice," he says quietly.

I nod.

He stands reluctantly and puts his phone in his pocket. "We'll have to do it again. I still owe you a coffee."

He doesn't really, but I only shrug and stand.

"See you around?"

"Something like that," I say, smiling.

After that, I take to going to the Gizmo at the same time on purpose. He bought me coffee the first time, but after that I've purchased my own. It felt too much like dating otherwise, and even though I've wondered if we could ever get to that point again, the thought of it is a little terrifying. For now I'd rather just be friends.

It's been a few weeks of this, and he's starting to feel part of my routine again. We continue to talk about safe subjects. Friends, classes, our practicing routines. I tell him I like to head to the practice rooms late at night because fewer people are there and I'm more likely to get my favorite spot.

I don't mention the other reason I like being there at that time.

As I said, I'm keeping things safe.

One night I'm in my favorite practice room at the far end of the hall. I've wrapped up my official practicing routine, the one I tell Professor Reinecht about, and have started with the messing around part. The only time I do this is when it's late—it's nearing midnight now—because I don't want anyone to think I'm not serious about what I'm doing. I don't know why I don't want anyone to hear these songs I carry around in my head, I just don't. I'm only playing around anyway.

Though, this sort of playing is a different kind of magic. It consumes me in a way I'm almost powerless to control. Sometimes, I feel positively eaten by it.

I finish the song and rub the ache out of the back of my neck, rolling my head. A soft rap at the door causes me to jump. There, through the little window, Erik's peeking in at me.

My heart starts pumping. I almost feel caught. As I slide off the bench and go to open the door, he gives me a sheepish look through the window.

"Sorry to bother you."

I step back to invite him in. He closes the door behind him. "That's what I get for telling you my schedule. Stalker."

He grins a bit and shrugs.

He's already told me he has a piano at his condo. Naturally. I know without him saying so that he came to the practice rooms specifically to see me. I'm not sure how I feel about that, but I can't deny I'm glad to see him.

"What were you playing?" he asks. "It was really phenomenal."

I press my lips together. How much did he hear? He has that look on his face like he wants to start going on about it. It's the same look Sam had when she caught me playing my own song once, way back in our junior year. I'm not even sure why I think of it like that—like I've been caught doing something bad. But when I play like that, it's so different from what everyone else here is doing. That can't be good. All it's going to do is show I'm a self-taught poser when what I'm trying to do is be serious about this.

"It was nothing. What are you doing here?" I didn't mean for that to come out as harshly as it did.

He looks a little taken aback. "Well, I..." he gives me that sheepish smile again. "I know I can't say I was just walking by, but that didn't stop me from coming anyway."

I'm softening again, now that we seem to be safely past the subject of my made-up songs. I cross my arms, but give him a smile.

"And you came because?"

He smiles and shrugs. "It's been a long time since we played together."

I glance at the piano. "Uh, yeah. It's been a bit."

"Do you remember Chopin's Sonata in B Minor?"

I give him a look. Of course I do. That one was our favorite.

He gives me a questioning smile.

I sigh and roll my eyes. "All right then. You first."

He grins wider and heads to the bench. I can't help but smile at him. I've missed playing with him, too. I drift to the piano and rest my hand on its smooth surface.

His hands hover above the keys, but he doesn't play. He glances up at me.

He pats the spot on the bench next to him.

I hesitate, then sit down.

He takes a satisfied breath and begins to play. That's all it takes. We're caught up in the music again, but that's not all. Or at least, it isn't for me. As we take turns playing, and even start to play a duet together, I'm caught up in all those old feelings of love I had for him. They've returned so strongly, I'm not sure they belong entirely to the past.

I feel a little swept out to sea. Erik is next to me and his music is all around me and my defenses are falling. It's alarming to realize he could walk right into my heart again, if he wanted to.

We finish our duet but don't say a word.

We don't look at one another.

We keep our eyes on the keys and our hands in our laps. I'm breathing a little too hard. He is, too.

"Ashley," he says softly, "I'm really glad you're here at Hartman."

I nod, keeping my eyes on the black and white keys in front of me. "I'm glad you're here, too." And I am.

I feel him looking at me. I slowly bring my eyes to his face. Everything else falls away. It's only Erik. And me. And everything between us.

243

He's holding my eyes and I can't look away. But I'm afraid because I think he's going to kiss me, and what then?

Still I keep my eyes on him. He leans slightly toward me. I should lean away or look away, but I don't. My heart leans to him, and I follow. As we slowly close the gap between us, I see in his eyes the same torment of longing and fear that I feel.

Our lips touch and I close my eyes. Something in me comes unlocked.

As we press tentatively against each other, a lump swells in my throat. I couldn't swallow it down if I wanted to. A small sob escapes my lips. He takes my face in his and kisses me more firmly, but so gently.

I kiss him back, but then we stop and we're embracing instead and I'm crying openly.

"God, sweetheart," he says, tears in his own voice. "I'm so sorry."

I nod and pull back to look at him, the tears running down my cheeks. His eyes are glistening too and he looks so pained I want to comfort him. I put my hand on his cheek and he looks at me earnestly.

"I didn't want to hurt you."

"I know."

"God, it was so awful," he says, his voice cracking. "I missed you so much. I swear I loved you. I'm so sorry I put you through that."

I kiss him again and we cling to each other. It feels like we're finally, finally mourning together the losses we both shared. Heart aching, I settle lower into his arms, my head on his shoulder as we rock together in silence.

As our tears slow, still clinging to each other, we start talking about the one topic we've avoided more than anything else. I tell him what it was like, holding nothing back. I tell him about going to his house to find it closed up. I tell him how humiliating the doctor visits were and how I couldn't bring myself to tell any of my friends what was going on.

When I tell him about the miscarriage and the D&C at the hospital, my tears start up again, and he holds me tighter and strokes my hair. Then I confess the worst thing.

"I didn't want to get rid of the baby," I say tearfully, "but I didn't want a baby either. It was... such a relief. You know?"

I feel him nod against me.

"I—" he begins, his voice tight. "That's kind of how I feel right now. I mean, I know you lost the baby either way, but my dad only said you weren't pregnant anymore so I thought you had an abortion. I'm so relieved that's not what happened."

I pull back and look up at him.

"I mean, I'm not glad you went through a miscarriage, but—"

"You thought I got an abortion?" I ask softly.

"I thought my dad made you."

I shake my head and he exhales in relief. He still looks pained though. "I know what happened is still bad—"

"No, I understand what you mean."

We look at one another, taking deep breaths. He holds my face in his hands, kisses my forehead, and looks at me earnestly. "I'm so sorry. Do you think you could ever forgive me?"

"I have." I shrug. "I already have."

"God, really?"

I nod.

He closes his eyes and exhales, pulling me into another embrace. We hang on to each other firmly. I exhale deeply. Crying with Erik has given me a deeper feeling of healing than I've ever had about this. And it's made me feel like the things that have been between us aren't there anymore.

He pulls back and holds my face in his hands again, caressing my cheeks. We look at each other openly, tenderly. Holding my gaze, he slowly leans in and puts his lips on mine.

I close my eyes and kiss him back. I'm falling so far. God, I feel like he's falling right there with me.

His arms tighten around me, and our mouths slowly open to each other. When I feel his tongue on mine, my heart starts to race. I kiss him deeply, slowly.

I remember this. I remember him. I remember the feel of his hands on my hips. All of it. Suddenly that five years feels like nothing.

Our kiss grows more intense. My blood is starting to sprint. I snake my hands into his hair and his hands press against my lower back. Everything in me is racing ahead. My whole body is tuned in to him, wanting him, carrying me away so fast.

I pull back. "Wait." I can't. It's too fast.

He stops, but stays close. He gives me an appraising look. He fears my rejection. I see it.

Heart pounding, I pat his chest lightly. I quietly disentangle myself from his embrace. "I think I'd better go."

He stays on the bench, watching me.

I pack my bag and throw it over my shoulder. I don't leave right away though. I stand there looking at him for a moment.

"Can I take you to dinner tomorrow night?" There's a bit of trembling under his voice. The question he just asked must feel as heavy to him as it does to me.

I glance down at the floor, thinking, then back up to that face I've loved for years and years.

I grip the straps of my bag. We're on the edge of something. I feel it.

"Okay," I say, pushing us over.

I realize he's been holding his breath, because he lets it out slowly. "Pick you up at six?"

I nod and pull a small notebook and pen out of my bag.

I think about giving him my number, but I'm not ready to reintroduce the phone into our lives. I don't really know what's going to happen next. I don't want to be faced with even the possibility of unanswered texts again.

I write down my address and set it on the piano, giving him the slightest smile.

Then I really do leave, a little bit hopeful and more than a little terrified.

There's no going back now.

Chapter 15

I'm still getting ready when there's a knock on my door. I check the little faux-antique clock on my vanity. It's only five-thirty. Wasn't he supposed to come at six?

My hair is down and dried after my shower (no small task, that) but I haven't styled it yet. At least I've put on my lip gloss and I'm dressed. I'm wearing a silk scoop-neck peasant top and slim, black pants with a low waist. I smooth my hands over the material at my hips and answer the door to find not Erik, but Sam and Jack.

No wonder the time was off.

"What are you guys doing here?" I open the door to let them in. They both know about the date.

"Moral support," Sam says, but Jack has a look on his face that gives me pause.

"And we wanted to meet him," Jack says.

"No," I say in a pleading voice. "Please don't do this tonight."

"What?" he asks innocently.

"The whole big brother thing."

"I don't know what you're talking about."

I sigh. He's full of crap.

"Want help braiding your hair?" A diversion.

"I'm wearing it down."

He and Sam look at each other with raised eyebrows.

"Oh, cut it out." I head for my bedroom. "I just want to look nice."

They follow me back, but don't say anything. I stand in front of my vanity and grab the big curling iron I've been warming up. Jack plops on the edge of my bed and Sam starts to separate a lock of hair for curling. "Make yourself useful," I say to Jack, handing over a brush. He gets up and takes it obediently. Most the time I curl my hair myself, but they've helped me get ready before enough performances that they know the routine.

They're certainly speeding things up, which almost makes up for the fact that they're here when I'm pretty sure I'd rather they not be.

I wrap the ends of my hair around the curler. "You have to hide in the bedroom when he gets here."

"Come on, really?" Sam rolls her eyes and gets the next section ready.

"I'm serious. This is hard enough."

Sam exchanges a serious look with me in the mirror. "You don't have to do this."

I release my hair from the curler and give the curls support while they cool. "Yes, I do." I look at Jack firmly. "So no funny business."

"All right," he agrees, but he doesn't look happy about it.

"You were the ones who told me it was okay to forgive him."

Jack shrugs. "Well, yeah. But you also said it was over between you."

I exhale in frustration, taking the next section from Sam and starting to load it onto the iron. "Is it really so crazy if it's not?"

He frowns at the back of my head and starts to brush a section, even though he's already done it once. "No. I just... don't want you getting hurt."

"I know," I say, softening. "But..."

I focus on the strand I'm curling in the mirror, not saying anything. Sam and Jack continue their work in silence, waiting. I let my hair out of the iron and hastily hold it to cool for a few seconds. Ignoring the strand Sam's holding out for me, I put the iron on the table and turn to face them.

"Look, I appreciate your concern. I really do. I love you for it. And if I do get hurt, I know who'll have my back."

"And who will be stuffing Erik into a piano," Jack says.

"But this is not helping me right now," I tell him firmly. "Please," I say to them both, softer now. "I just need to do this alone, okay?"

Sam sighs and gives me a hug. "All right. I had a feeling this would be too much."

Resigned to it, Jack pulls me against his chest and plants a kiss on the top of my head. "I'm sure you'll have a good time." I don't think he's sure at all, but I appreciate the gesture anyway.

After they leave, I finish the curls, pondering things. I understand why they're afraid. I'm afraid too, and of the exact same thing. But I can't ignore the way it felt to be with Erik yesterday in that moment when there were no more barriers between us. My heart felt snug inside of his.

It felt right.

I have to see where this goes.

That right feeling began again the moment he picked me up—looking so smart in a button-down shirt and loose slacks—and has carried on all the way through dinner. We're at The Iron House, a tiny upscale steakhouse on the north side of town, sitting close in the circular booth. It didn't start this way, but over the course of the evening we've been slowly drawn into each other. We're facing slightly toward one another so we can look into each other's eyes as we talk. His arm is around my shoulders and I'm holding his other hand. Our hands rest lightly on my thigh.

The waitress cleared our plates and took care of the check long ago, but still we linger. We've talked about so much, I couldn't go back and list it all if I tried. Right now he's finally touched on the topic of his dad.

"It's hard to resolve how I feel about him, you know?" he says quietly. "How do you try to settle something with someone who's gone? Sometimes I'm just <u>so</u> mad at him, but other times I actually miss him. Even though he was really hard to deal with sometimes, he wasn't all bad. I did love him."

I nod in acknowledgement, not wanting to interrupt.

"At the same time, I can't seem to let go of my anger. At least with my mom, I've been able to kind of talk through things. Though we didn't really talk about what happened with you until after the accident."

Then he starts to tell me what it was like to take care of his mom right after it happened. She was lucky to survive, and it was a rough haul there for a while. From what he says, she'll never be all the way back to normal. I stroke his arm again as he talks. It sounds like it was a pretty tough time for both of them.

When he mentions she's living here in Rosebrook, I ask in surprise, "She moved here?"

He nods, absently playing with my hair. "It was the only way I would agree to go back to school so soon. I wanted to be able to check on her, or help her out if she needed it. She insists she doesn't need help anymore, but I think she knows that's not true because she didn't really fight me on it. She was just glad I was willing to come back to music. She was afraid I'd left it for good."

"Why would you do that? Because of the accident?"

He sighs and cocks his head. His eyes cast over the restaurant before coming back to me. "Juilliard was... not what I thought it would be."

I raise my eyebrows slightly.

"Or at least," he continues, "the music world was a little more harsh than I thought it would be. It's just so competitive, you know? And so few of us can actually make a career of it. The more I learned about the odds and what I was up against, the more I started to realize the path I was on was something that had been decided for me. There was never any question. No one ever asked me what I wanted. It was just assumed. I was good at it, so of course that's what I'd do. And there I was, years later, neck deep in the bowels of Juilliard wondering if that's what I even wanted."

I can only blink at him. I can't imagine someone with Erik's passion questioning any of this.

"Then the accident happened. I was already accepted into the graduate program at Juilliard and still had another couple months on the lease of my apartment. My parents were in San Antonio by this time. Another promotion for my dad," he explains with a wave of his hand. "Anyway, I flew home after the accident. Mom thought I was going to go back to school after the funeral. Maybe at first I thought I was too. But when I left New York, I realized I kind of wanted to be away for a while. Figure out what I wanted, now that my dad wasn't there to tell

257

me what I wanted. And there was just so much going on with my mom, you know? She was such a mess. Physically and emotionally."

He pinches his brows together and looks down at our entwined hands. He rubs one thumb over the back of my hand. "I know this might sound a little cold, but sometimes I think my dad dying was better for my mom." He looks back up to me. "She'd kill me if she heard me saying that, and would probably deny it. But she's a lot softer now. Without him."

"Maybe that was from being so injured, instead of from being without your dad."

He shrugs, furrowing his brow and getting the slightly angry look that seems reserved for his dad. "Maybe. But he was so... domineering and controlling. He always had to have his way. No matter what. No matter who it hurt."

He takes a deep breath and I start stroking his arm again.

"Anyway, even with all the distraction of what was going on with my mom, being away from music became painful. Like, physically painful. I eventually realized I really <u>did</u> want a career in music, more than almost anything." His eyes get that burning desire I recognize in myself. "No one was pushing me anymore, but I wanted it. I wanted it more than I ever wanted it. Without it, something in me felt…"

He pauses, looking for the right word.

"Empty?" I suggest. We share a look of understanding. Two kindred souls who know what it's like to have something like music living inside you.

He nods. "Yes."

"I'm glad you didn't leave music behind. What a waste that would've been."

He gives me a gentle smile. "I'm glad I came back too, but not for that reason." We smile at each other softly. "At least," he says, "not <u>only</u> for that reason."

"Because you missed your music, didn't you?"

"I missed you more." He leans in and gives me a gentle kiss that swirls up a whirlwind in my chest. "I was empty without music," he whispers, "but I've been more empty without you."

259

We stay until the restaurant closes. I'm still not ready to leave him yet. I don't think he's ready either, because he invites me to his place to see his piano. It's actually the same one we used to play on together, so I've already seen it.

But that's not why he asked me over and that's not why I agreed.

He lives in a charming townhouse on Herma Vista. It's not as grand as his parents' old house on the Boise River, but it's nicer than any grad student apartment I've ever seen. On one side of the entryway is a sunken area, with a comfortable-looking living room set and a flat screen TV. On the right, a staircase leads to the second floor. Holding hands, we go through a short hall to the rear of the house. A kitchen with a bar opens onto the family room opposite it. There's a set of large windows that I assume give a view of some kind of backyard, but it's too dark out to see. The family room has a couch and a chair, a stone fireplace, and, of course, the piano.

I smile as we walk up to it. I rub my hand along its smooth surface and exhale slowly. "I've always been in love with this piano."

He snakes his arm around my waist and pulls me to face him. My heart does a little flip when I look into his deep brown eyes. "If I didn't know better," he brings his hand to my cheek, "I'd be jealous."

He kisses me then, and it's the kiss I've been waiting for. We kissed many times at the restaurant, but this is different. We're alone now, and safe, and truly in each other's arms at last. We slowly inhale together as we sink deeper into an embrace. My heart is thumping soundly. Mouths opening to each other, our tongues gently touch.

Under my cascade of hair, his arms tighten around me, one hand curling around and cupping my shoulder. The length of our bodies press against each other. I bring my fingers into his hair, and our kiss deepens.

As we taste and caress each other, I don't just want him physically, though there's that too—my body temperature is climbing with each passing minute. I want <u>him</u>, the man I loved and... God, it's happened so quickly, but I can't help it... the man I love again.

Our kisses slowly escalate to a new intensity. He backs me up slightly until my rear hits the piano. His firm erection presses against me. He lowers his mouth to the crook of my neck and I soften in his arms, my head falling back. When he comes back to my mouth, our kisses are heated and hungry.

We sink to the floor and he lowers his weight on me. I hook one calf around his leg. We kiss each other passionately, breathing hard between each kiss. As I rub my hands along his body, he feels so familiar—like coming home—but also slightly changed. He's a little firmer and broader in the chest. His presence above me is more substantial than it had been. It only makes me need him more.

I wrap my legs around his waist and his shaft presses hard into me. Tremors of pleasure ripple under his touch in response. He slides my shirt and bra strap off my shoulder in one motion and sucks on the exposed skin. I arch my head back and pull up the hem of his shirt until I can rub my hands on his bare back.

I bring my hands to the front, caressing his abs and chest. He lifts up slightly and together we remove his shirt. He comes down and claims my mouth, his hand sliding under my bra. Wanting my shirt off as well, I indicate I want to roll over and he follows my signal. Hanging on to each other, he rolls onto his back, keeping me close in a strong embrace. Sitting up and straddling him now, his desire strains underneath me. I pull off my shirt and slide it down the length of my hair before tossing it away.

I'm wearing a deep purple, lacey bra. Eyes taking me in, he gently slides both hands down the length of my breasts as I reach behind me to release the hook. As soon as the material springs forward, he takes hold of it and pulls it down my arms. He drops it to the side slowly. Still breathing hard, his eyes glide between my chest and my face a couple times, before his eyes lock with mine.

When he holds my eyes and sits up, my breath catches in my chest. He wraps his arms around me and kisses me so deep and so slow, I think my heart's going to break.

He slowly pulls me back down, until I'm lying on top of him and my hair is falling around us in sheets. Looking into my eyes, he brings his hands to my face. For a moment it is only this space, and only he and I in it.

"Oh, honey," he whispers. "I missed you so much."

"I missed you, too. I've never stopped missing you." I kiss him with as much love as I've ever felt for him. He kisses me back, holding me close.

Three more heartbeats and the softness is gone and the fire is back. We're kissing each other so feverishly, I'm slightly dizzy. Hanging on to me, he rolls me onto my back, then starts planting hot, wet kisses down the length of my neck. The electricity on my skin increases steadily as he advances to the crook of my collar bone. When he hits the bullseye, I let out a shaky exhale and shudder with pleasure.

He keeps going down, until he's eagerly working my breasts. He teases and sucks my nipples and I arch against him, needing more. He finally releases me to suck on the tender skin just below my breast. As he works his way down my stomach, I start to throb, anticipating him.

I hook my thumbs under my waistband and shimmy my pants down my hips. He kneels back enough to help me slide my pants off, but doesn't take his eyes off my lacey panties. He pulls the wet crotch away to reveal my folds. He takes one long, hungry lick from my opening to my clit and I arch back, bringing my knees up.

"God, Erik," I breathe.

His tongue caresses me softly and my eyelids flutter shut. His tongue slides over me masterfully. My arm flies out to the side and my outstretched hand presses flat against the floor. I'm panting and moaning shamelessly now. One hand runs up my bare stomach and to my chest, cupping and squeezing me.

I'm throbbing and aching to be filled. "I want you."

But he doesn't stop. He slides two fingers into me and I grab his hair, pushing him against me. He massages my breast and I gasp for breath. My legs start to tremble. My chest flushes hot. He thrusts his fingers in and out of me, sucking on my bud and then working his tongue over it in circles.

Oh my god. I can barely breathe. As I climb to a hard peak, my body tightens and strains for release. I gasp again, then moan. It feels like my whole body is ready to burst. He curls his fingers slightly, hitting my G-spot, and I convulse, exploding into an orgasm. I cry out, the blood rushing in my ears, as he massages me and keeps me coming.

I fall back, arching my neck as waves of pleasure crash over me. My eyes flutter open and shut, giving me brief glimpses of the ceiling and the underside of the piano. I'm clutching at the piano leg, half gasping, half crying out. Just as I start to come down, he gives me one, long, shuddering suck on my clit and pulls his fingers out.

I exhale sharply, looking at him. "Little devil," I breathe.

I'm positively aching for him now. I can see by the glint in his eyes, he did not forget that little trick.

He pulls his pants down to his thighs and his bulging cock springs loose. I did not forget this man's length or girth, and am torn between wanting to take him into my mouth and wanting to take him, period. Before I can reach for him though, he rolls slightly away so he can kick his pants all the way off.

I slide off my soaked panties. He comes back to me and I hook my arms around his neck. Like he's got some sort of built-in homing device, his tip is at my throbbing entrance.

He pulls back sharply, moving away from me.

I make a sound of protest.

"Sorry," he says, breathing hard himself, "you'll have to wait while I take care of things."

He starts to get up but my arms and legs tighten around him, keeping him in place. "Honey, I've been on the pill for <u>years.</u>"

He blinks. "Right." He pauses for a moment, giving me a heavy look of understanding.

"Don't think. Just kiss me." He does, and drops his full weight on me. His full shaft slides in and we exhale deeply together, tucking our heads toward each other.

My whole body tingles with satisfaction at having Erik once again. "I've missed you so much," he whispers again.

But I can't answer, my brain momentarily paralyzed by pleasure as he pulls out, then slowly rocks into me deeper. "Yes," I say softly, my hands gripping his shoulders. He slowly pulls out and slides deeply into me again. God, what sweetness.

As I tuck my nose into the crook of his neck, his arms tighten around me and his hand cradles the back of my head. As our movements pick up speed, the hot breath of our rhythmic pants mingles together. Still cradling me, Erik steadily increases the pace and power of our lovemaking until it rises like a crescendo. We rock together as if we were one. I'm like a taut string, vibrating with the slightest touch.

I'm climbing closer and closer to the edge. The muscles in his back grow tighter as he climbs too. He wedges one hand under my ass, angling me slightly. The tip of his shaft starts hitting me in that deep pocket of pleasure, over and over.

I let out a long, low cry, sharp bursts of pleasure pushing me up and up and higher and—my breath catches—<u>over</u> into a heart-stopping climax. He thrusts into me deeply and groans as we come together. I throw my head back, riding the waves, clawing at his firm back.

He thrusts into me rhythmically as my clit releases measure after measure of pleasure. When it's over and I'm flushed cheek to chest, our embrace softens. We're rocking ever so slowly now. He rubs his nose across my cheek. He kisses me and our tongues caress each other softly. Finally, we come to a stop, pressing firmly against the other, still fully joined.

We stay that way for a moment, neither one willing to pull away from the other. At last we release together into a puddle of flesh and bone.

Chapter 16

I spent the night at Erik's. It's fast, and a little scary, but I can't seem to step back. I don't think I want to. We stayed in the rest of the day rediscovering each other, sometimes naked, sometimes not, and thoroughly enjoyed the novelty of not having to worry about getting caught by anyone. I'd probably be there still, except he has a standing appointment to have dinner at his mother's house every Sunday. We both acknowledged that if things continue on with us—and there's no doubt in either of our minds that we want just that—we'll have to get our parents in the loop.

It's too soon for that though. When he dropped me off at my place, I texted Sam and Jack to see if they'd want to watch a movie tonight, then cleaned up and headed over.

When I get to Sam's apartment, she's sitting on the couch with her legs crossed. The second I walk in the door she takes one look at me and says, "Oh my God, you slept with him."

I stop in my tracks. "What the hell? How did you know?"

"I've literally never seen you smile like that."

My cheeks flush as I shut the door behind me, but it's true. I can't stop smiling. I go over and plop on the couch next to her, letting my head fall against the back.

"Good Lord, you're practically swooning."

"Shut up." I grin.

"All right." She turns to me eagerly. "I want details."

So I tell her. I don't give her the juicy details, but I tell her everything else. By the time I'm done, she smiling at me contentedly.

"I love this," she says.

"You do?"

She nods and I smile. "Me too."

"Have you told the girls yet?"

I shake my head and pull out my phone. I've been keeping Chloe and Isabella apprised of things along the way, but I hadn't had a chance to tell them the absolute latest. "What about Jack?" I ask as I'm typing. "He seemed pretty concerned last night."

"Eh." Sam waves her hand. "He just has that male protectiveness thing going on right now. It'll pass, don't worry."

After I get Chloe and Isabella up to speed, I toss my phone on the couch cushion and sigh with satisfaction. Sam is still grinning at me.

"God, you're really lost to him, aren't you?"

"Not lost." Sam has a funny way of talking about love sometimes.

"Found then," she says dramatically, batting her eyelashes.

I laugh. "That's better."

"Does this mean you're bringing him on the couples trip to the resort? Because you're way fucking overdue for getting laid on a couples trip."

"Hey!" I say, a little taken aback. Sam's always taken it upon herself to be the little sex cupid of the group, but ever since she found out about what I went through in high school and the unhealthy way I'd tried to cope with it once I started college, she's kept me out of her crosshairs.

"Oh come on. I haven't been able to harass you about sex for <u>years.</u> Fucking <u>years.</u>"

"It's been a trial for you, has it?" I raise my eyebrows.

"Damn right. But now that you're back to banging the guy who got you pregnant, all bets are off."

My mouth drops and she gives me a wicked grin.

I can't help it. I start laughing. How does Sam get away with this shit?

"So this is what I want to know." She leans forward, eyes glittering. "Is he hung?"

"Yeah, I'm totally not answering that."

"Just show me with your hands. This big?" she asks indicating.

I roll my eyes and make a <u>pffft</u> sound.

"Bigger?" She gapes at me.

273

I don't answer. All I can do is try to suppress a smirk, and try not to get too wet thinking about Erik's cock and all the things I did to it last night.

"Oh my God, you struck gold, baby girl. Dick like that is worth waiting for, am I right?"

I get up and head for the kitchen. "I liked it better when we had an understanding." But I'm smiling. It makes me feel better to know Sam isn't treating me with kid gloves any more.

As I'm pilfering a few chocolate chips from the open bag in Sam's freezer, Jack arrives with drinks and snacks, plopping the grocery bags on the kitchen island. She's followed him in and has started peeking in each bag to see what he brought.

"What are we watching?" Jack asks, taking three beers out of the case and stashing the rest in the fridge.

"Empire Records," Sam says. This is another movie we've watched so many times, we could practically recite the whole thing.

She makes a face and lifts out a little package of Nutter Butters, just far enough for me to see, before dropping it back in the bag. No one likes them but me.

"Mmm." I pluck them from the grocery bag, still grinning like a lunatic. I can't help it. "Thanks Jack."

Jack gives me a one-armed hug and plants a kiss on the top of my head. Rather than let me go though, he holds me close. "How'd your date go last night?"

"Good." I grin up at him.

He's wearing the same concerned big brother expression he had last evening.

I squeeze him. "Really good. It's okay, I promise."

He glances at Sam, who gives him a reassuring smile. He sighs and kisses me on the forehead before releasing me. "If you promise."

"I do." Sam and Jack grab some snacks and we all grab a beer before heading into the living room. I plop my drink and snack on the floor and sit cross-legged in front of the DVD player so I can load up the movie.

"Now Ashley has someone to bring on the couples trip," Sam says, plopping in one corner of the couch and tucking her feet under her. Jack sinks down on the other side.

"Sam," I warn. "I haven't even asked him yet."

She shrugs.

I roll my eyes and look at Jack, who's studying me carefully. "I haven't even asked him yet," I repeat lamely.

He cocks his head at me. He looks at Sam and they have one of their weird, silent conversations I've seen them have before. He looks back at me and I give him an exaggerated, silly smile. He laughs and his expression softens.

"See?" Sam nudges him with her foot. "She's happy."

"Yeah, okay."

"Well, I'm so glad you approve," I say sarcastically, sticking out my tongue.

He breaks out into his goofy Jack grin. "You should be. How could you ever go on if I didn't?"

I roll my eyes and return my attention to the player, putting in the disc.

"So now everyone will have dates," Sam says satisfied.

I glance over at her. "Who are you bringing?"

She shrugs. "I don't know. It's, like, five whole weeks away."

Well, I guess that's true. Sam and Jack both tend to rotate through partners more quickly than that.

Although...

Now I'm the one giving Jack an examining look. Come to think of it, instead of hearing Jack talk about a slew of girl companions, like he usually does, we've really only been hearing about Peggy for a while now.

Seeing me, he gets a sheepish look on his face.

"Who are you bringing, Jack?" I grin at him.

"Peggy," he answers shyly. God, how adorable.

"If she's still around," Sam says easily.

"Well, um, I hope she will be. We actually, uh, well last night we kind of... um..."

Sam's giving Jack a perplexed look, but I'm still grinning.

"Dude," Sam says. "Spit it out."

He leans back into the corner of the couch and throws his long arm over the back, trying to look casual. "Last night we decided to be exclusive."

Sam's jaw drops. I have to work to suppress a laugh. I can see Jack needs encouragement, not teasing. "That's great. This is a first for you, right?"

"Damn near." He gives Sam a nervous glance.

She claps her hands to her chest in delight. "Our Jack is finally in love," she teases.

"God." He shudders, "who the hell said I'm in love?"

This time I do laugh. Oh, this is going to be fun, I have to admit.

"Jack and Peggy sitting in a tree," Sam teases. "K-I-S-S-I-N-G."

"Seriously?" He gives her a flat expression. "That's the best you got?"

"First comes <u>love,</u>" she continues, grinning. "Then comes <u>marriage.</u>"

As I watch him react to two trigger words right in a row, I see Sam's teasing had more teeth than it first appeared. His expression of exasperation causes us both to laugh.

He rolls his eyes.

"Oh leave him be."

Apparently satisfied, Sam relents and crawls over so she can give him a kiss on the cheek. "Ah, our little boy is growing up."

He groans as she leans against him, putting her head on his shoulder. "If you guys get married, do you promise to make me your best man?"

He pinches her side, causing her to squeal and jump. "Hey, you brat!"

"Fair's fair," he says, but she settles against him again.

"So why didn't you bring her over?" I ask.

He raises his hands in protest. "Let's don't go nuts. Are we going to watch the movie or what?"

Sam and I exchange amused looks, but we let it go. I push play and lay back on the floor, resting my hands on my stomach. As we get into the movie, my eyes are on the screen and I'm even tapping my foot to the music, so I suppose I'm technically watching.

But truly, my mind and heart are far away with someone else.

And I can't wait until he gets home.

The following week, Erik and I fall into a new pattern almost without talking about it. We chat in the Gizmo between classes. We practice at his place every afternoon and into the evening. We make love whenever the fancy strikes us, which is often, and I fall asleep in his arms every night. I've accumulated a fair amount of clothes and toiletries there already, and the spare toothbrush I bought gets more use than the one at my apartment.

When Chloe asks, as part of a group text with the girls, if I've moved in with him, I reply: <u>No. That's a little too much too fast.</u>

What's the difference between that and what you're doing now? Isabella wants to know.

"Commitment," is what I think to myself. While I'm trying to articulate the difference,

Sam answers for me: <u>The difference is she can still run.</u>

So, basically the same thing. Not that I want to run from Erik, and I hope to God he isn't planning on running from me, but I'm not ready to think much past today. Not yet.

This weekend, Erik and I are enduring another separation, but this one is my doing. A few weeks ago, my parents bought me tickets to fly back to Boise so I could spend the weekend with them. It's been a while since I've been home, so it's nice to be here in our familiar kitchen. I think even the cat missed me, because she's curled up on my lap, letting me pet her. Either that, or she's getting too mellow in her old age to protest.

The relaxed mood in the kitchen changed once I started telling them about seeing Erik on campus. I decided to tell them the story from the beginning, hoping it'd be easier to take if they could see how everything's unfolded, but as soon as I get to the part about asking Erik to tell me his side of the story, my dad interrupts.

"Wait," he says, frowning. "Are you back together?"

Boy, he put things together quickly. I really wasn't at that point in the story yet, but my face betrays me.

"After what he did to you?"

"Robert," my mom warns. She wasn't exactly happy with Erik either, but she didn't seem to hold a grudge the way Dad has. Or the way I did. Not that I fault either one of us.

"Will you just listen?" I ask.

He makes a gesture to indicate he will, even if he doesn't want to. I rush to fill in the rest, eager for him to forgive Erik like I did once I knew what happened, and to stop looking at me like he thinks I've been taken by a sleazy con artist or something. By the time I'm done, my dad is rubbing his forehead, looking pretty unhappy about how it's all come back full circle.

"Poor Erik." My mom leans on the table on her elbows. "I feared it might have been something like that, but I sure wish we'd known at the time."

I think again about how hard it must have been for Erik to have his own family working against him when he was still so young.

"Okay, that's all well and good," my dad says, looking at me firmly, "but do you really think it's a smart idea to start things up again?"

My defenses come up. Between my dad and Jack, this is getting ridiculous. I'm not a little girl who needs protecting. I'm twenty-three. I can make up my own mind. "Why wouldn't it be?" I'm trying to keep my voice controlled.

"Look, you guys aren't kids anymore," he says, in a tone that suggests we're still acting like it. I furrow my brows in frustration. "You're at an age where things have the potential to mean a lot more. For any relationship you're in at this point in your life, you need to ask yourself what kind of future you have together."

"Robert," my mom says, trying to soothe him.

"No, really." He refuses to be reined in. "It's hard enough for concert pianists to have any sort of meaningful relationship because they're on the road all the time."

I try not to roll my eyes at him. Why is he saying this as if I don't already know? I'm the one who freaking told him what it's like for people in my field.

"What chances do you have if you're both on the road? Not to mention all this history you have."

"We just barely got back together, Dad. Slow down." I'm still not ready to think much into the future, and this isn't helping. Things with Erik are amazing, but they're also incredibly intense. I can't ever seem to get enough of him and he seems to feel the same about me. Taking it a day at a time is all I can handle right now. "I wish you would just... be happy for me."

He sighs. "I just don't want you to get hurt again."

"Don't worry," I say a little petulantly, tired of having to defend my relationship with Erik. "I'm on the pill."

He gives me a look. "That's not what I mean."

"Well what <u>do</u> you mean?"

"What's going to happen if one of you decides it's just too hard and isn't going to work?"

I frown. I can't know for certain the future of our relationship any more than anyone can know the future of <u>any</u> relationship. I don't have a crystal ball. What does he want from me?

"I'm an adult now," I say at last. "Let me worry about that."

As much as I hate to admit it, my father has planted a sliver of doubt I haven't been able to completely remove. Practicing for the upcoming regional competition is keeping it fresh in my mind. There <u>are</u> complications with us being in the same field. But it isn't the travelling lifestyle of concert pianists I worry about the most, although there is that. It's the fact that we're both always going to be competing against one another for the precious few opportunities in the world of professional pianists.

The truth is, the Myra Hess Piano Competition is just the beginning.

On the other hand, the fact that we're going to be competing against one another is going to be true whether we stay together or not. Neither one of us is going anywhere. And if I'm going to compete against him on stage, regardless of the outcome, I'd rather go home in his arms afterwards than not.

I've decided to keep these concerns largely to myself, for now at least. First, because it's my hope that they're fleeting. I was able to live in Erik's shadow before, so I should be able to do it again, even though the stakes feel a lot higher now. Second, it's my problem, not his. I'm the one playing second fiddle, so I'm the one who has to make peace with it. Erik's only ever been encouraging, and that's no different now. Why should I lay all this on his shoulders?

In some ways, the whole situation is a vortex of swirling emotions vying for attention: I'm deliriously in love with him and relieved to have him back in my life, I'm terrified to face him in the competition, and I'm just as determined to win as I've ever been. I just keep thinking about the possibility of performing at Lincoln Center, and that pushes me to try harder, against all odds.

As we practice together, even if I'm able to hide my little doubts, there's one thing that's clear to us both: I'm desperate to win, and so is he.

That doesn't stop us from taking the inevitable break from practice and winding up naked on his living room floor or in his bed and going at it like our lives depended on it. If I had any sense at all, I'd practice on my own more than with him. Here at his place, he's a bit of a distraction.

But when have I ever had sense when it comes to Erik Williams?

Besides, we're making up for lost time.

Chapter 17

My last class let out only an hour ago, and I already find myself in Erik's bed once again. I have one leg thrown up over his shoulder, and am watching the muscles in his firm chest all the way down to his pelvis as he thrusts into me without mercy. This is the raw, animal side of Erik that reminds me he's not a kid anymore.

I'm not a kid either. I'm crying out shamelessly, my face drawn in an expression of pleasure that would put even porn stars to shame. Everything about him gets me hot: his sexy body, his impossibly gorgeous face, his spell-bounding music, his tender declarations of love. Sometimes I just want to consume him.

He pulls out and indicates he wants me to turn over. I obediently get onto my hands and knees, arching back to meet him. My long braid falls to one side—we didn't bother undoing it—and I brace myself as he enters eagerly. Overcome with the pleasure of him inside me, I drop onto my elbows and drop my head at the same time. He's filling me up and lighting my core on fire and it's still not enough. I still need more.

I rock back against him hard, angling myself so I'm open even more. He grips me by the shoulder, and his sack starts hitting my swollen bud.

"Yes," I breathe.

I drop onto my chest, my ass curved up sharply. I start to tighten around him, approaching the tipping point.

"Look at that pretty, little ass." He slaps my ass hard, then grabs both cheeks and spreads them slightly, working us up toward the peak. The pleasure in my body is so high I can't believe I haven't come yet. I grip the sheets with both hands and press my face into the mattress, stifling my cry as he rides me higher and harder.

Finally, I break and I'm thrashing and shuddering. He comes with me and we both cry out, riding our joint orgasm unhindered by any self-consciousness.

I'm in the grips of it for a long time, but eventually I'm limp and panting, with Erik coming down from his high too. He comes out and lies down next to me, partly lying on top of me.

We take a few moments to catch our breath. I turn my head so I can look at him and we both break into broad grins.

"Holy shit," he says. "You're like a little sex goddess."

I laugh a little, still panting. "I don't know about that, but having sex with the grown-up you is a completely different experience."

He laughs, all low and rumbly. Someone should put that on a CD, because I could listen to it over and over again.

His arms pull me in closer and I adjust so we're lying chest to chest. I exhale deeply, my body sinking into that relaxed state that goes clear to my bones. He caresses my cheek and kisses me gently. "I love you, sweetheart."

I smile and my heart jumps. I haven't tired of hearing Erik say those words to me, and hope I never do. "I love you, too."

We sink into a deeper embrace. My body is getting heavy. I feel a delicious post-sex nap coming on.

He lightly trails his fingers along my back and arms. I can tell he's wide awake, but I'm so sleepy and relaxed I can barely move. He lightly kisses my cheek. "Will my playing bother you?" he whispers.

Eyes still shut, I shake my head slightly. We're approaching the time in the day we reserve for him to get in an uninterrupted practice session. My slot's a little later. Plenty of time for sleep.

He kisses me again and gently extricates himself, tucking me snugly under the covers and giving me one last kiss on the cheek. Just as I'm drifting off, his music comes up from downstairs and I smile, surrendering myself to sleep and his music at the same time.

Later, as I'm nearing the conclusion of my own practice session, he comes in from the study where he's been doing some homework and slides onto the bench next to me.

I wrap up my song and give him a kiss. "Just a few minutes more."

"Will you play your song for me?"

"What song?"

"The one I heard you play in the practice room before. Remember?"

I do remember. I remember being a little mortified that he'd heard it. I still don't know how much he heard. Hopefully just the tail end. "I don't play that for people."

"I'm not people."

I don't answer.

"Come on, it's just me."

I don't know if I can. My heart has started to pound and I'm not even sure why.

He takes my hands in both of his. "Please." Then a slow smile blooms on his face and my breathing shallows. How I love his smile. He kisses me gently, still holding my hands.

"Please?" he says again, carefully letting go of me and sliding off the bench. "Okay?" He's smiling but watching me, like he's trying to keep me in place just with his eyes. It's working. He lays down on the floor, looking up at me.

"For me?"

I sigh. <u>Dammit.</u>

He gives me a satisfied smile, knowing I've given in.

I look at the keys. <u>It's just us,</u> I tell myself. No one else has to know. I'm not playing for my professor or anything ridiculous like that. I'm just playing around, and Erik will understand that.

In the next second, I change my mind.

Then I change it back again.

Oh, hell.

I practically attack the keys, beginning the song with too much gusto but needing that to get me started. Soon, the music becomes what it's meant to be and that magic thing inside me happens and it's only me and my music. There's that little flutter of fear in my heart—the only evidence that part of me knows I'm playing for someone on purpose, and not because I got caught—but playing my own music has a unique power over me. It draws something out of me that's wild and vulnerable. When I'm able to tap into it, it surges through me even more than the great classical compositions do.

It's practically blasphemous.

When I'm done, my heart is pounding so soundly in my chest, I think it's going to break loose. I'm always a bit overcome after playing like this, but now that I've stopped playing, that flicker of fear I felt earlier has returned as an inferno and is violently competing for space in my heart.

I grip my hands together on my lap and glance at him nervously. He's sitting up cross-legged now, with a stunned look on his face.

Okay, this is why I don't play my own stuff for people. It's one thing to be critiqued on how I'm playing fucking <u>Bach</u> or something brilliant and centuries removed from where I am now. I don't know if I can handle a critique on something so personal.

"If you don't like it, I don't want to know."

He blinks and shakes his head sharply. "What the hell are you talking about? Ashley, you're practically handing me this thing."

"Handing you... what thing?"

"The Hess Competition. Why in the hell aren't you playing that?"

I scoff. If I didn't know better, I'd think he was trying to sabotage me. Not that he would. Not that he needs to. "It's just..." I don't really want to talk about this. "It's nothing."

"Nothing," he says flatly.

I frown and cross my arms at him.

He blinks at me, as if he's had some sort of revelation. Then he frowns too. "Seriously Ashley? You're still doing this shit?"

"What are you getting irritated for?" I ask, pretty irritated myself. "I didn't play that so you could give me crap about it."

I get up from the piano and head for the kitchen, not even knowing what I need in there. He gets up to follow me.

"Why are you hiding your talent?" he says, and I cringe. "I don't get it."

"Hey, I'm hardly hiding my talent. I've won my fair share of competitions too, you know."

"I'm sorry, but playing like that in secret like you're some teenaged boy jacking off in the shower"—I spin on him—"is absolutely hiding your talent."

"You know, I don't really need advice about it from someone like you."

"Someone like me?"

My heart's pounding like a cornered animal. Why can't he leave me alone about this? "Yes. Someone like you. You have no fucking idea what it's like to try to compete with people like you, who've had the benefit of professional training your <u>entire freaking lives.</u> I think I'm doing just fine keeping up, if you want to know the truth, so I'd appreciate it if you'd stop giving me shit about what I do or don't play. I've got enough things getting in my way."

He cocks his head at me, like he's seeing me for the first time. His anger drops away immediately, but the intensity of his expression hasn't changed at all. I cross my arms in front of my chest protectively. "Let me tell you something, Ashley. Lack of money and opportunities aren't what's getting in your way. The only thing getting in your way is your own head. Because when you can get past whatever your hang up is well enough to let loose, you're a fucking goddess on that thing, doing shit no one at Hartman or anywhere could ever teach you. So stop blaming me and everyone else for your problems and play that damned piano like I know you can."

My arms are still crossed and I'm still frowning at him, but I'm blinking back stunned tears. I can't unhear what he's just said.

His expression softens and he comes up, putting both hands on my shoulders. I still can't move. He's stirred up a storm in me and I can't push it down. I'm trying, but I can't make it go away.

"Don't be afraid to show people what's inside you." He gives my shoulders a squeeze, puts a soft kiss on my forehead, and quietly leaves me to deal with the aftermath alone.

After dinner, I head back to my place for a change of clothes. Erik hasn't pushed me any more about the matter—other than to say he thinks I should change my piece for the regionals—and we've managed to rather soberly recover.

But as I gather my things together for another couple nights at his place, the silence of the apartment is shattered by my song lilting around in my head.

<u>Am</u> I handing this competition to him? But having the gall to play my own piece feels far too risky. In seven days we're heading to regionals in Seattle, where I won't be up against just him, but the best in every music conservatory in the west. Only three pianists will advance to the finals in New York. If I want to be one of them, I can't afford to screw around.

His words come back to me: "Don't be afraid to show people what's inside of you."

I know he's at least partially right. I always pour my heart into my playing, but when I play raw and powerful like that, I expose myself in a completely different way.

Playing that way on stage couldn't feel any less vulnerable than if I were up there playing completely naked.

But I'm afraid of more than that, I know I am.

What is it? What am I afraid of?

I don't know for sure, but suddenly the thought occurs to me that I'm afraid to be too good. It's a rather terrifying thought, so I must have hit on something. I don't understand why that should frighten me, but it does. Part of me thinks, that kind of success can't be me. Things like that don't happen to people like me.

I can't be as good as he says.

But there's this other part of me that can hear the music just as well as Erik can.

I think of his stunned expression when he heard me play, and that's how I feel sometimes, too. Stunned. I'm not completely sure where such music comes from, even though it's coming from me.

Maybe that's part of what scares me, too. Maybe if I set it free, really get it out there and take a chance on it, it will disappear and I won't know how to get it back.

I sigh and sink to the edge of my bed.

I know Erik's right. I do hide like I'm ashamed of it. But I'm not sure I have the courage to do anything else.

On impulse, I pick up my phone and dial Sam's number.

"Hey stranger," she answers jovially.

But I'm not in the mood to play. As I fill her in on what happened, and my thoughts about it, she listens quietly. When I'm done, she says simply, "Go for it."

My heart pounds at these words from her. "I don't know. I don't know if I can. Or if I should."

I hear a sharp exhalation from the other end of the line. "Have you talked to Isabella or Chloe about this?"

"Uh, no. I just called you."

"Why me?"

I blink. What kind of question is that? "Because you're my friend."

"Of course I am, but so are they. Out of the three of us, why did you call me?"

This gives me pause. I could say it's because she's here and they're not and I talk to her about lots of things first. The realization of the truth, though, is starting to settle in my stomach. I'm not ready to let it solidify yet. I'm still trying to hold it back. "Um... because you're the only one I knew would be up?"

"Bullshit. It's fucking nine o'clock."

Yeah, I know, I think. I'm grasping.

"I mean, because you're the only one who's heard me play like that. I thought maybe you could... I don't know."

"I'll tell you why. You called me because in spite of being kind of a chicken, you <u>want</u> to go for it and you knew that's exactly what I'd tell you do to." And there it is. "So do it already."

I grip the phone. I feel like I've been tossed around in the storm Erik stirred up inside me, and just like that Sam pulled me into the eye of it, where everything is eerily calm and certain. And deadly one foot in any direction.

She's right, though. I <u>do</u> want to go for it. I want to go for it so much I'm starting to suspect I'm <u>actually going to do it.</u> I'm so terrified I can hardly breathe.

"So are you going to play your song or not?" Sam demands.

"Okay," I whisper.

Sam doesn't chastise me for such a weak pronouncement of intent. She doesn't tell me to yell it out like I mean it, like we're in some made-for-TV movie or something.

She just says, "Atta girl. Give 'em hell, Ash."

Chapter 18

It turns out, it was past the deadline to change songs for the regionals. When I told Erik that, almost like an excuse, he nodded resignedly and hasn't said another word about it.

When I sit down at the piano on stage at the regionals, I hesitate, as if there's some question about which song the judges are expecting to hear.

That storm Erik stirred up. It won't calm down.

It's so nonsensical, I can't help but wonder if I'm about to self-destruct.

I've been sitting here too long. I can tell by the heavy silence settling over the audience. I can hear the shuffling of feet. Someone coughs softly and every person in the house can hear it. I look up to see Erik in the wings. He couldn't possibly know what

I'm thinking, but then again, maybe he does. He looks at me firmly and raises one brow, like he's egging me on.

Fuck.

I look back at the keys and raise my hands. All I have to do is make myself play the first note and then I'm committed. Then the rest will come.

I pause, then with more boldness than I've ever possessed in my life, I play the first note of the composition I played for Erik. It's a composition I haven't even been brash enough to name yet.

But named or not, it's making its debut right here in Benaroya Hall. As I play the first measure, my blood is pounding through my body. My fingers are a bit unsteady, and I miss a note. Though no one knows the composition, it's an off note and I know it had to ring false in the ears of the judges, even if the audience didn't pick up on it.

Push through it, I hear Professor Reinecht saying in my mind.

So I do. I get through another measure without a mistake. And another. I can't believe I'm really doing this. It's like I just kicked myself out of the competition on purpose.

I'm too terrified to look at the audience. I'm too terrified to look at Erik. But another two measures and I hit a place where I could fall into the rabbit hole of my own music, if I wanted to.

Fuck it.

It's a split second decision, but in that instant I'm truly all in. If I'm going to play my song, I'm going to fucking play it.

Like it or not, these people are going to hear me.

Just like that, it's only me and the piano and my music and I surrender to it. As the music rises to a crescendo, I'm rising slightly off the bench, letting the rapture of it come through on my face. I'm the master of those goddamned keys. I command them to bring forth the music that burns through my soul and they obey.

I play the last measures, my fingers flying across the keys, and when I play the final note I straighten and look at that magnificent piano. That's right, baby.

The next half second takes a lifetime.

305

I'm back in the hall. The storm is gone. It's only me left raw and naked on stage and—I'm certain—absolutely fucked.

It's as if time itself has stopped. I'm stuck forever in that half-second pause between the end of a piece and the audience's reaction.

Or maybe it's not really a half-second pause at all. Maybe it was such a crass display of self-indulgent ego, they can't even bring themselves to clap.

My eyes land on a woman in a flowered, satin top. Her mouth is partway open and she looks like she's been mowed over by something. Then, like it's all happening in slow motion, I watch as her hands float up and her face breaks into a smile.

The applause that explodes in the auditorium crashes over me like a tsunami.

I startle and time catches up again. Everyone's clapping and cheering and... getting to their feet.

They're getting to their feet!

I'm getting to my feet as well, but it's not really me doing it. It's my training taking over. I give the audience a gracious smile and a bow and the cheering swells even more. I walk off the stage, but I'm going in the wrong direction. I'm supposed to exit stage right, but I go stage left. My legs are trembling and I'm not sure I can make it.

What did I just do? What the hell did I just do? Did I really, really just do that? WHY would I do that in the middle of a competition? This was my chance to play in Lincoln Center. What the hell was I thinking?

I leave the stage and stop in the wings, not knowing where to go or what to do next. The few people on this side of the stage are either ignoring me or blinking at my dumbfounded expression. I don't know how long I'm standing here, but soon Erik's heading over from backstage rear—he must have gone through from the other side—and beaming at me. He takes me into his arms and spins me around. I'm too stunned to protest.

He's laughing in my ear, all warm and rumbly. That's what brings me back from whatever out-of-body place I've been. I cling to him fiercely.

He sets me down but I continue to hang on, afraid my legs are about to give out. He takes my face in his hands. "Magnificent. God, that was so fucking magnificent."

Then just like that he's kissing me with such gusto I can't believe he's doing it right in front of everybody.

I pull away, still hanging on to him. "I can't believe I did that. What if I just disqualified myself?"

He shakes his head and holds me firmly by the shoulders. "Honey, the worst they'll do is dock you some points."

"That's almost as bad. Every point counts."

But he just smiles at me. "Oh Ashley. Promise you'll still love me when you're famous, okay?"

"I'm supposed to be over there," I say stupidly, pointing to the wings on the other side of the stage. "I was supposed to play Debussy. It's in the program, Erik. Oh God, what have I done?"

He puts his arm around me, leads me to a chair, and sits me down. "Here." He pulls one of those mini water bottle they've been giving us out of his front pocket. "Drink this."

"Is there vodka in it?"

He laughs. "Come on, honey."

I take off the cap, my hands shaking slightly, and take a small sip.

He kneels in front of me, his hands on my thighs, and holds my eyes. "Deep breath," he says steadily.

I take a deep breath, not taking my eyes off him. My heart rate is starting to come down some. My panic is starting to recede.

He nods in approval. "Again."

I take another deep breath.

"Did you hear the way the audience responded to you," he says, not as a question.

A fluttering starts in my chest. It was good. I'm starting to realize, what I just did was good.

"They were <u>on their feet </u>for you," he says, smiling.

They were. They were on their feet. The fluttering in my chest swells until it feels like I have giant butterflies inside me, threatening to carry me up to the sky.

A slow smile starts to bloom on my face.

His eyes glitter at me. "Don't you dare regret this."

Still tentatively smiling, I say, "I played the hell out of that piano, didn't I?"

He throws his head back and laughs. "Yes, you sure did. How did it feel?"

"Amazing. Incredible. Even better than when I play it for myself." I couldn't say why. For most of it I forgot all those people were out there.

Not to mention the judges.

My smile fades a bit. If I'm not, in fact, disqualified, the judges are required to dock me points for switching songs. I can't imagine the rest of my score will be high enough to make up for it. Forget coming in first, or even third. At this point I'll be lucky not to come in dead last.

But...

My smile creeps back on my face. "I played my song for them," I say slowly. "I really did it. And they liked it."

He's smiling and nods at me.

Even if I just knocked myself out of the competition, I <u>don't</u> regret it. There will be other competitions, but <u>this.</u> This is a moment I already know has changed me forever.

There's still a part of me that's terrified, but this new part of me is braver than I ever thought I could be.

And I think she's here to stay.

Chapter 19

The next weekend we're at the Rivers Paradise Resort in Swan Pointe for our long-awaited couples trip, and it can't have come too soon. Ever since I placed first at the regionals, just barely knocking Erik into second place, things have felt a little weird. No one was as shocked as I was when I won, but as the week has worn on, I've wondered if Erik's the one who's reeling. I don't think he's used to losing, least of all to me. Sometimes I think he's bothered, but the next second I wonder if I'm just imagining things. I can use a break from it all, and hope this trip will be the perfect antidote.

Isabella and her husband, Shane, flew in from Boston for the weekend. Even though Chloe and Grayson live in Swan Pointe, they seem to be off travelling more than they're home. They got back from a trip to the US

Virgin Islands just in time to drive from their house, up the hill to the resort, and to meet us all in the grand lobby. Jack broke up with his girlfriend after a record nine days and didn't bother finding anyone else to bring along. That wasn't terribly surprising, but it <u>was </u>surprising when Sam decided to fly solo too.

"After the way things went the last time I brought some guy on a getaway with me," she'd said wryly, "I'd rather just keep my eyes open for possibilities once we're there."

When we were first planning the trip, I think Chloe and Grayson suggested all of us going down the resort's zip line just to mess with Sam—"No fucking way," she'd said—but after the insane-sounding roller coaster zip line they did in Florida a few months ago, I have to wonder if regular zip lines aren't up to snuff for them anymore anyway. Just watching the video of it they put on their YouTube channel made me queasy.

Isabella and Shane don't seem to care what we do, so long as they're with each other. It's heartening to see how happy they are together.

Tomorrow is our big group activity—we're going whale watching—but today it's been lounging poolside most the day, then seaweed wraps and massages at the resort's luxury spa. After that little activity, I was torn between wanting to lure Erik up to our room for the perfect happy ending and being too relaxed to blink.

We had dinner at the resort's five-star restaurant and have since wandered our way into the lounge for after-dinner drinks.

The second we walked in and spotted the sleek grand piano on the far side of the room, Erik and I exchanged longing glances. We've been holding off though, not wanting to abandon the group completely. We've found an arrangement of soft couches and chairs to settle into. I'm in a long, flowing skirt, high-heeled boots, and form-fitting top. Erik's looking especially hot in black slacks, a soft gray shirt, and a casual dinner jacket. I could eat him up right now if I weren't so full from dinner.

"Hey you guys," Grayson says to Erik and me, "when's your big performance in New York again? Chloe and I are trying to

314

figure out if we can coordinate things to come watch."

"That'd be great!" I say.

Chloe nods enthusiastically. "I'm afraid it might conflict with the Wine and Chocolate Festival though. We've already committed to that one. I'd love to be there for you, though."

"Yeah, I've never seen Ashley perform," Grayson says. "You either, of course," he says, looking at Erik.

"It's not really a performance. It's a competition." I hear the tension in Erik's voice, but see no evidence of it. He looks relaxed enough. Then I notice him clenching his hand slightly. Well, maybe he's relaxed.

Grayson smiles good-naturedly. "Yeah, but I thought it'd be better not to mention that part, you know."

"Because these two love-birds will be going for each other's jugulars?" a grinning Sam says, in typical Sam fashion.

"I don't know that we're going for each other's jugulars," I try to say lightly. I'm not sure I'm pulling it off.

315

"Well, there can only be one winner," Erik says, with a wink. We're both smiling, but I feel the heaviness underneath our words. Or am I just imagining things on his part?

I really need to stop obsessing about it. But lately I've been worrying more than ever about how the constant competition will affect us in the long run, especially now that I'm closer to actually <u>being</u> his competition.

I stop that train of thought before it goes any further.

I want to believe we won't let that kind of thing come between us.

I have to believe it.

I give Grayson and Chloe the date for the competition, then grab Erik's hand. "Come on, we've ignored that piano over there long enough."

It's been awhile since we've improvised together, but last time we discovered a rhythm we liked so much we came back to it a few sessions later, repeating and building on it. I wasn't willing to think of it this way at the time, but we basically composed a song together.

"Let's play this one." I slide onto the bench and tap out a few notes to remind him. Our composition doesn't have a name I can call it, but I decide it needs one—just like all the other ones I've written over the years. "We should call it the Nutter Butter song, because that's what we were eating when we wrote it."

"You're both nutters if you like that crap," Sam says, coming up to us along with the others.

"Hmm." He's only half smiling, and keeping his eyes on the keyboard. "That's not a very serious title."

"That's why I like it." I grin and nudge him with my shoulder. Come on, I think, relax with me.

He settles his hands over the keys, and I do the same. I glance at him nervously— trying and failing to stop reading so much into everything—then we get to it.

It turns out that's all that was needed. As we play our song, any tension there was between us—real or imagined—is gone.

Ah yes, this is more like it.

317

I suddenly feel like I don't have a care in the world. It doesn't even bother me when I catch Sam recording us with our phone. I just make a face at her, smile, and keep going. I have Erik to thank for that transformation. Not all that long ago, I would've been <u>mortified</u> to see Sam recording me.

By the time we're done, we've drawn the attention of other patrons in the room. With some encouragement from the bartender, we keep going. This time we opt for pop songs—an easy transition since our composition is a fun blend of classical and rock elements—and get our little group singing. When we start playing <u>Crocodile Rock,</u> patrons from elsewhere in the bar start to gather to us and join in the singing as well. By the time the song is half way through, it seems the whole room is singing along. Well, who can resist a little Elton John?

Next we play <u>Piano Man</u>, <u>Don't Stop Believing</u>, and even <u>Bohemian Rhapsody</u>. In between songs, Erik and I sneak in a little flirting—a pinch on the side here or a kiss on the neck there. That gets me as light-hearted

318

as anything else. This is what I've needed. When we finally exhaust ourselves and the patrons both, my arms are tingling pleasantly from playing so much, and my body is more than tingling from wanting him so much.

As our group leaves the lounge, Erik's arm is snug around my shoulders and mine is hooked around his waist. We keep giving each other little squeezes. Everyone says their goodnights and we return to our fifth-floor room that overlooks the city and the bay.

The curtains are drawn from the windows, letting in soft light from the full moon. We don't bother turning on the lights. He plops on the end of the bed, then collapses all the way back. Smiling at him, I pull off my boots then climb on top of him. Straddling his lap, my skirt hitched up to my thighs, I smile at him.

"Mmm," he says in the most delicious way, his hands caressing my thighs. "I thought you might be too tired."

I shake my head. "Are you too tired?" It's not a serious question. I feel him growing beneath me.

"Oh yeah." He runs his hands from my thighs to my hips. He presses down on me with his hands while pressing his hard cock up against me. Good lord, I love how fast he's ready for me. "I'm way too tired."

"I can tell." My hands run down the length of his arms as he slowly brings his hands up my sides and to my chest. Even through my shirt and bra, his touch makes me tingle.

Caressing me gently, he gives me a soft smile that gets my heart doing tricks. "Have I ever told you how much I love you?"

"And my breasts," I tease.

"Yes. Those beautiful breasts, too."

He slides his hands under my shirt so he can caress me properly. I tuck my bare feet under his thighs, settling firmer into his lap. Together, we press against one another.

"Have I ever told you how much I love you?"

"And my cock."

"Yep. That too. So yummy."

He laughs slightly and I smile broader. I slowly lift my shirt off. He looks at me hungrily, still slowly caressing me.

I come down on my hands, my hair falling in a sheet on one side, and press myself against his cock again. I let out a soft exhale at the pleasure of him against me. His eyes close briefly and his hands go to my hips.

Meeting my eyes, he rubs his hands up my back then gently unlatches my bra. I lift first one hand, then the other, as he slides it off my body and drops it to the floor. He eyes my full breasts, and supports their weight, gently rolling my erect nipples between his fingers. I give another soft exhalation of approval.

I nuzzle into his neck, keeping my back arched to give him free access to my chest. I place a hot breath on his bare skin, then taste him slightly.

"Mmm," he says softly.

He starts pulling my skirt and panties down until my bare ass is exposed and my panties are stretched by my open legs.

He squeezes my ass, spreading me slightly. I throb in response.

I kiss his warm lips and taste his tongue. As we kiss, I lift my hips and first one knee, then another until my skirt and panties are on the floor too. I'm naked and straddling him while he's fully dressed. Something about that gets me even hotter.

He gives my ass a firm slap and I kiss him deeper. His hands curl around the back of my thighs, heading for my wet seam, but I break our kiss and start to crawl backwards, taking myself out of reach.

"Tease." He grins at me.

"I don't know what you mean," I say innocently, but my look is wicked enough.

Having scooted past his lap, I sit up on his legs and look at the promising bulge in his pants. I rub my hands up his thighs, watching the anticipation building on his face. Ever so slowly, I reach his cock and give it a firm squeeze through the material.

He exhales, his eyes shutting briefly.

Encouraged, I unfasten his belt and pants, pulling down the front of his silk boxers until his sizeable shaft is set loose.

I take him in both hands and lean down. He gathers the hair cascading next to me, and takes hold of my shoulder. Positioning my mouth over his broad shaft, I don't close around him until I'm almost as far down as I can go. My tongue and mouth make contact, tasting him at last. As I work my way back up to the tip, gently sucking, he groans and squeezes my shoulder.

I flick my tongue against the underside of his tip, then slide my mouth down his shaft again. My hand pumps the base with short, firm movements. As I continue to work him, I sneak looks at his face. He alternates between throwing his head back with his eyes closed, and looking down at my mouth around his cock, his lips parted in pleasure. Spread over him, I'm aching for his touch.

His cock pulses in my mouth, responding to my efforts. "Damn, girl," he breathes. "Get up here."

He doesn't have to tell me twice. I give him one last, slow suck back to the tip, then break loose and his cock springs up.

I scoot up until I'm directly over his cock. I lower myself onto his hard shaft, exhaling at the pleasure of him filling me at last. Bracing my hands on his chest, feeling his muscles through the soft fabric of his shirt, I lift up slightly and back down again. My bare legs rub against the material of his pants.

He grips my hips, helping with the movements and breathing heavily. He starts to finger my nipples. Sighing, I sit up and arch my chest into his eager hands.

Riding him, my channel is stretched and humming with pleasure, but my clit is throbbing and untouched. I arch back more, my hair brushing his thighs. He removes his fingers from my nipples. When they return, they're slick with his saliva. I groan with approval.

Our eyes meet and my heart clenches, burning for him as much as my body is. He gets his fingers wet again. I wedge my knees slightly wider, hoping. His fingers dip down and I bite my lip in anticipation. When he slides over my hard bud at last, I shudder, my mouth working into an O. His cock is at its deepest inside me at the same moment.

He moves his fingers in circles, his other hand gripping my hips firmly. I brace my hands on his chest again. I scramble the material of his shirt up until I meet bare skin. I spread my fingers wide. His thrusts grow

324

harder and more intense. I fall on him, our bare stomachs touching. He embraces me firmly as we give each other a hungry kiss.

I prop myself on straightened arms, changing the angle of his cock as he comes hard into me. He sucks my breast, squeezing my ass as I ride him. "Yes," I gasp. He sucks me harder, flicking his tongue against my nipple.

"God, Erik."

"You're so tight, baby."

"I'm so close," I manage to say, pinching my eyes shut and feeling my cheeks get hot. "Don't stop."

His fingers get some of my moisture, then rub against my opening stretched around him.

I build toward my peak, letting out one short gasp after another. He fingers my rear opening. The tip of his finger penetrates me slightly and I climax hard over his engorged cock. Almost losing control of my ability to move, he maintains our rhythm as I contract on top of his fully-dressed body.

When I'm spent and lying weakly on top of him, he runs his fingers lightly up my exposed back, eliciting a shiver. I'm still wrapped around his hard shaft, only the occasional aftershock making me contract around him. He caresses his fingers down my back, around the fullness of my ass, and along the back of my thighs. Light tingles awaken under his touch.

He slowly pulls his erect cock almost completely out of me, then slowly slides back up my sensitive channel. I throb slightly, responding to the promise of more.

He pulls out, rolls me onto my back, and gets off the bed. Our eyes stay locked together as he slowly removes his jacket. They stay locked as he discards his shirt. He drops his pants to the floor and my eyes fall to his cock, still exposed and ready. By the sight of it, more than ready.

He crawls panther-like onto the bed. Gently taking me by the hips, he rolls me onto my stomach. I'm stretched out like a cat, legs together. He straddles me, his knees on the outside of mine. His erection finds the tight gap between my upper thighs. I arch my ass back to meet him, spreading only slightly, and his firmness finds its way.

His dick rubs back and forth along my folds. He kisses my neck, my shoulder blades, my upper arm.

Sliding one arm under my collar bone, so he's embracing me from behind, he rolls me onto my side. From behind, his cock is still rubbing along my folds, but now I can open to him. I lift my top leg and bring my knee back so I'm hooked around his hips. He reaches down and guides his cock inside me. I moan.

Once he's in and the angle's secure, he starts rocking me from behind. He rubs up my stomach and chest to my neck. He cups my jaw and turns me to face him enough so that he can kiss me. We kiss soft at first, then our tongues dive deep as he picks up his rhythm.

We release our kiss and I face forward again. His arms are around me and his cheek on mine. I bring my upper knee back just a little, opening more to him and bringing him in deeper. I hold onto the arm embracing me, then bring one hand behind to rub his lower back and ass.

He squeezes me and pinches my nipple. I tilt my head back and hold his cheek as he kisses me again. His hand trails along my stomach, dipping lower. I throb, wanting him.

When he hits my slick bud, I bring my knee higher. Pumping me, lower arm cupping my breast, free hand circling my clit, Erik plays me like the master he is. We moan together, building. Our movements grow faster and his cock stretches taut. This time, he's mine, and the anticipation of feeling him come inside me increases my pleasure.

He hooks his arm under my leg, then strums my clit firmly. My body starts to convulse. His face is next to mine. He's breathing hard with me, holding me tight, his slick fingers increasing their rhythm to a frenzied pace. He's ramming me furiously. He kisses my cheek. And again.

Then I come undone. He continues to work me as I orgasm hard, gripping his arm and digging my nails in. I'm out of my mind with pleasure, consumed by it. Consumed by him. It goes on and on, and it's not until I'm riding powerful waves downward that he finally comes. He clutches me to him and groans in my ear. His thrashing climax brings more pleasure in my body, and I contract with it again and again.

At last we slow and start to relax, bodies humming with the afterglow. He removes his hand from my satisfied bud and hugs my thigh to him before releasing my leg back down. I sink deeper into his embrace, pressing my whole body against him. He embraces me firmly, and we kiss slowly, deeply, him still resting snug inside me.

When I face forward again, we roll slightly so I'm even more wrapped up in him. His leg drapes softly over my hips. I sigh contentedly and close my eyes, feeling this moment of unity and safety is its own little eternity, and that our world now and forever will be only he and I, together.

Chapter 20

His mother has known about us for some time, like my parents, but today is the first day I've joined them for their Sunday dinners. I was waiting for an invitation, not from him, but from her. After two months of dating her son, I finally got one.

Erik tried to warn me about Lydia's physical appearance. As I only remember the polished, coifed woman from my childhood, I'm unprepared for the change anyway.

The most glaring remnant of the accident that killed her husband is a series of broad scars on the right side of her face. Her right cheekbone is slightly lower than the other one, cracked during impact. Less visible, but no less lingering, are her internal injuries. Her back was so damaged she walks slightly hunched, suffers from chronic pain, and still can't lift her hands above her shoulders. Her right lung was so damaged she's had periods where she's needed oxygen. This is not one of those times, but her breathing is a bit shallow and labored.

Just as striking is the overall change to her presence. There's barely a hint of the powerful woman who'd so intimidated me as a girl.

Lydia shakes my hand upon arrival and gives me a smile. We arrived early in the day so we could help her with some things she can't take care of herself. Though she does have some help that comes in weekly, there are things she and Erik both seem to prefer he do for her himself.

We spend a few hours on various chores, I help Erik prepare dinner, and the conversation stays on safe topics: school, current events, movies.

At the conclusion of dinner, after so many hours in her home and in her presence, I'm glad I came. It wasn't as bad as I feared it might be. I think I'll start coming more often, if they want, so I can help too.

When we're about ready to go and Erik's dismissed himself to the restroom, things take a subtle turn.

"I understand you're competing against Erik in the Myra Hess Competition."

There's a slightly hard tone to her voice— this, I remember—but it's so slight I'm not sure it's really there.

"Well, we're both _in_ the same competition," I say calmly, "yes."

"You beat him in the second round." Now I'm more certain about the accusatory tone I hear.

"He beat me in the first," I say, holding my ground.

She takes a sip of her gingerroot tea. She moves slowly, the cup trembling slightly. I feel guilty for a moment. I'm ready to go into battle with this frail, broken creature. What am I thinking?

"Did Erik tell you he almost quit music?" She puts her cup on the wooden table with a soft thud.

I nod. "I'm glad he didn't. It would've been such a waste."

"He had to come to grips with the kind of competition he faces at his level." She looks at me meaningfully. My cheeks grow warm. If I'm about to be pulled into battle with her, it's not entirely my fault.

But in the next moment, her expression softens.

"It's clear you care for my son. But I'm not sure it's wise for him to have this sort of competition in his personal life too."

I take a soft, steadying breath. It wasn't just the competition, it was the controlling way they raised him and him needing time to figure out his own mind. I keep those thoughts to myself and address her comment instead. "We're very supportive of one another."

She nods, as if she agrees, but she shrugs one shoulder. "I hope it works out, Ashley. For both of your sakes. I just worry it might be too much for him."

I look at her, not sure what to think. I can't tell if she's being the meddling woman she's always been, or if she's just expressing fears that, after all, I also have myself. Getting comfortable with a high-level of competition is not the same as wanting it in the middle of your intimate relationships, and most professional musicians don't. But whether her concerns (and mine) are valid or not, I can't help but feel resentful—for my sake, but even more for Erik's. All he's ever wanted is for his parents to have his back, the way my parents have mine.

"Well," I say, gently but firmly, "I'm sure with the support of the people we love most, those challenges will be a lot easier to manage."

She glances at me in surprise, then gives me a thoughtful look.

Erik returns to the kitchen and we take our leave without saying another word about it.

A mere week later we're back stage at Lincoln Center. I'm torn between being in awe of where I am, and too focused and full of nerves to really appreciate it. Erik is by my side, holding my hand. We arrived in New

York yesterday, and spent the evening at a romantic restaurant and going for a stroll.

It was a nice evening, but the closer we've come to the finals—this moment—the more I've felt we're on the edge of something.

For the first time, there's no certainty about which one of us will place higher. Not that either one of us are in a position to assume victory. As big as this competition is, we could both go home with our tails between our legs.

The musicians who have played before us are phenomenal. I don't envy the judges their jobs.

But this isn't just about the competition. Though I've tried to quiet my fears about it, there's no denying it now. This is also about us, and our future. Are we crazy for even trying this?

I take a deep breath and Erik squeezes my hand. I look at him to find his expression far away. His brows are furrowed in what I hope is just pre-performance concentration. He's looking toward the stage but doesn't seem to be seeing it.

I look away and take another breath. I need to stay focused too, and not feed my worries about how this may or may not affect our relationship. One step at a time. We can only do this one step at a time.

I start to mentally run through my piece—another one of my compositions, which I titled <u>Top of the Bridge</u> when I submitted it to the judges—and feel myself getting into a better frame of mind.

I want to win this competition. I want it so badly, I'm not sure I'll be able to keep it together if Erik wins.

Though... if I'm going to lose to anyone...

But that's not where my mind needs to be.

I need to think like a winner. So I do.

Erik goes first and captivates me with the magic of his music, like he always does. The audience responds well too, giving him a standing ovation. From the wings, I clap enthusiastically, equally proud of him and terrified he just secured himself the victory.

When he comes back stage, he's both beaming and holding back, like he doesn't want to boast. I hug him tightly. "You're so fucking good," I say in his ear.

"We'll see if it's good enough." He pulls back and gives me a kiss. "My biggest competition is about to go out. Are you ready?"

I nod and take a shaky breath. I don't allow myself to analyze him, or us. Not now. I have to stay focused. Whatever happens, we'll have to deal with it then. I try to ignore the part of me inside that's shaking.

He releases me just as my name is announced. "Good luck."

I don't answer. It takes all my concentration to walk onto the stage of Lincoln Center like I belong there.

I must say, now that I'm out on this magnificent stage, the experience is divine. Exhausted as I am from worrying about me and Erik, I allow myself to get swept away by the wonder of what I'm doing. Lincoln Center. God.

As I bow gracefully and settle at the bench, I look at Erik backstage. He's focused on his phone's screen, holding it up like he's going to take a picture or video of me.

Just when I thought the experience of being in Lincoln Center couldn't get any better, I begin to play. And I've never played so well.

It's pure rapture.

Gone are my doubts about playing my own music and really letting myself go. I'm all in now. This is what I was built for, right here. God willing, this is what I will spend my life living for.

When it's over, I have no idea if my score will end up on top or not, but I know I've done my absolute best.

I look up to smile at Erik, but he's not there.

Chapter 21

A chill drops through my heart. I face the audience, bow to their standing ovation, and resist the urge to check the wings. Surely he'll be there. I'll see him when I get back there.

The audience is still clapping. I hold out one arm gracefully, bow again in gratitude, and make my way to the wings.

Back stage, he's nowhere to be seen. I glance across the stage to see if he's on the other side, but he's not there either.

Ignoring my pounding heart, I start looking for him. By the time I confirm he's nowhere in the backstage area, my panic increases and my mind begins to race. What happened? I consider, and reject, a series of possibilities. Maybe he had to go to the bathroom. But during my performance? Maybe he got a call? But why the hell would he answer a call then? Besides, I saw him silence his phone when we got here. Maybe he started to feel sick?

I exit into the rear hallway and start checking rooms. Most are locked, but the ones that aren't are either empty or holding performers who aren't him. Gathering my wits about me, I find my coat and pull my phone out of the inner pocket.

There are a few good-luck texts from the Firework Girls and my parents, but nothing from him. No missed calls. I don't bother texting, but call instead. It goes straight to voicemail.

I send a text instead: Hey babe. Where'd you go?

I take a deep breath and try to calm down my heart. He's here somewhere. He wouldn't just disappear.

I wrap my arms around myself, pushing away the memory of the last time he disappeared on me.

He's here.

I find the men's room and wait outside. After fifteen minutes go by, I stop the next man about to go in and rather pitifully ask him to see if Erik's in there. When he confirms what I already knew, I go back to my coat. I force myself to put away my phone—even though I've been compulsively checking it—and return to the wings.

Maybe he's back now anyway. Maybe I missed him before somehow. But he's still not there and the last performer has had her say. The stage hands direct us onto the stage so we can receive the results. As instructed earlier, we all line up.

All but one.

The emcee is in front, holding a thick, cream card that I assume tells him who won. I glance to both sides of the stage, hoping to see Erik in the wings.

Nothing.

God, what on earth?

A cold chill drops through me. Something's wrong. Erik wouldn't miss this unless... unless...

The words of our parents hit me full force. His mom was worried he couldn't handle this kind of competition in his personal life. Hell, even my dad has been worried about the same thing. I knew before Erik even came back into my life that moments just like this can be death to relationships. I've known it all along. Was I kidding myself that we could be the exception?

The audience bursts into applause and I look out in surprise. The emcee is smiling at me. The short woman next to me elbows me softly. "Go on."

My brain catches up to me. My name was called, but for what? Did I place? Did I win?

As I move forward, a woman comes from the wings—still no Erik on that side—and presents me with a bouquet of roses and a medallion, which she puts around my neck.

Good lord, I think I just won the whole thing. And Erik is still nowhere to be seen.

I'm smiling, and there's this little underneath part of me that's thrilled, but the rest of me is reeling. Somehow I manage to get through it and we all exit the stage and that's that. The auditorium is filled with the low rumbling of an audience that's just been dismissed. It's a strange, perfunctory conclusion to something I've been working toward for months.

I receive congratulations from my fellow performers, still wearing the mask of a smile on my face.

The full realization of his absence sinks into me. Indignation starts to bloom. Did Erik just leave me? Again? Fucking, just like that? What excuse could he possibly have for this?

But then I remember thinking once before that there was no excuse for what he'd done. Only there <u>had </u>been an excuse.

I take a deep breath and straighten, free from the well-wishers at last, and head for my coat. I don't know what's going on. I don't know what's happened. But I'm going to believe in him. I trust him.

I start checking with the stage hands and organizers to see if they know anything. I call the hotel to see if he's there, but turn up empty. I exit the building and start checking the grounds. I go past the reflection pool and head toward the main plaza. Being nighttime, it looks different than the last time I was here, four months ago with my Firework Girls.

Erik was on my mind even then.

Struggling to keep my fear at bay, I go all the way to Columbia Avenue, looking around for him.

He's here. He's somewhere. He hasn't abandoned me.

I keep telling myself that, determined to believe it. I'm as fearful for us as I am fearful for him. What if something horrible happened to him?

I can't imagine what. What horrible thing could have happened in the wings of Lincoln Center?

But there has to be an explanation. I just need to find him.

Turning up empty, I go back to the reflecting pool. I just need to stay put. For all I know, he's looking for me too and we keep missing each other.

I check my phone again. Nothing. I sigh in frustration and put it away. Maybe his phone is dead. I don't know.

I should reasonably wait by the entrance to Lincoln Center, but patrons are still slowly exiting the building and I'm too easily recognized. I've tucked the medallion into my bag but I still have the bouquet of roses.

I decide to keep an eye on the building from a distance. I'd rather wait and worry in private.

I approach the base of Illumination Lawn and climb to the top, just as I did last summer. When I get to the rail at the back, I take in the massive white building that is Juilliard. The lights within glow. It's quite lovely. But the building doesn't have that other-worldly aura it used to.

It used to represent this out-of-reach dream. It used to mean I wasn't good enough, not really. But tonight I just proved there's more than one path to success, and Juilliard doesn't own it.

But Juilliard also represented Erik. It still does.

And that's what finally gets my tears flowing. I can't stop them. I'm terrified. I'm terrified for him and for me and for us.

But I can't stop believing. He's somewhere. He'll come to me. He's somewhere.

I scan the sidewalk below and all along Juilliard. I consider going across the street to see if he's there, but if he's looking for me too, it'll be at Lincoln Center. I have to stay put.

Just before I turn back so I can check the crowd coming out of Lincoln Center again, I hear his voice from far away, calling me: "Ashley!"

My heart leaps into my throat and I spin, my eyes searching frantically. I hear him again—this time a little closer—"Ashley!" I see him! He's running across the plaza, coming from Lincoln Center.

Heart pounding, I run down the slope of the lawn, the cool air hitting the tears on my cheeks.

When we reach each other, I drop the flowers and he takes me into his arms, lifting me off my feet and clinging to me.

"Where have you been?" His voice is muffled in my neck.

"Me? Where have you been? I've been looking all over for you!"

He sets me down and looks at me with concern. He looks pale and worn and I instantly know something horrible did happen.

"I'm sorry, honey." He wipes the tears from my cheeks. "I didn't mean to scare you." His eyes glitter and he smiles at me through the weight of whatever's happened. "You won. God, I'm so proud of you. I'm so sorry I wasn't there for you."

Now I'm more confused than ever. "How do you even know that? Erik, what's happened?"

His smile drops and he takes a shaky breath. "My mom's in surgery."

"What?!"

"She was having a hard time breathing. Well, harder than usual. Her lungs were filling with fluid. They almost lost her in the ambulance."

My head's spinning not only from what he's saying, but from wondering how he knows any of this.

"She's in surgery now. Just before my phone died, I gave Margie your number to call when Mom gets out. Did she call you yet?"

I shake my head, still trying to get a handle on everything. "Who's Margie?"

"Mom's neighbor. She checks in on her from time to time. She found mom on the floor, trying to get to her phone to call 911. Once she called 911 with mom's phone, she texted me with hers. It came in when I was recording you, otherwise who knows when I would've seen it. I saw it was an emergency and went into the hall to call. The paramedics weren't even there yet. I was listening as Margie talked to 911, and then once they got there she kept me up on what was going on."

"My God. Is she going to be okay?"

He nods and shrugs wearily. "I think so. Before she went in, the doctor told Margie she should come out of it all right."

I shake my head. What timing, with us clear across the country and our flights not for a couple more days. "Are we flying back early?"

Now it was his turn for tears to come to his eyes.

"Oh, honey," I whisper. Poor guy. It's been a rough night for him, too.

He blinks them back. "Yes, I'd like to. I was hoping you'd be all right with that."

"Of course."

I hug him and we hang onto each other tightly. "God, we must have kept missing each other," I say. "I thought—"

But I don't say what I thought.

He pulls back, a look of dawning on his face. "You thought I left you?"

"Just... for a moment," I say helplessly, shrugging. "I kind of thought about before, you know?"

He looks confused. "But... for what reason? Why would I leave?"

"Well..." I hesitate, but realize I need to just come out with it. Maybe I should have a long time ago. "Because we're competing against each other, and maybe that's more than you want in a relationship. You wouldn't be the first musician who felt that way."

He sighs. I instantly see I haven't been imagining his unease since I won the second round.

"Look, I know I've been licking my wounds a bit. I mean, yeah, I'm not crazy about losing to anyone. But that's not about you, sweetheart. You can understand that, can't you?"

I sigh. "Well, yeah. I didn't handle things too well when you beat me in the fall."

He grins sheepishly.

"But, is this going to come between us eventually?"

He takes my face in his hands and kisses me. "If I'm going to lose to anyone, I'd rather it be you. Yeah, there's that selfish part of me that hates to lose, and I'd be lying if I said I don't hope I can beat you in some other competition someday." I can't help but smile. "Wouldn't you feel the same way?"

God, I would.

"But I'm also so proud of you and so fucking crazy in love with your music."

His words bounce around in my heart in recognition. Does he really feel that way about me and my music?

"God, honey, when you play like that you make me fall in love with you all over again."

I smile broadly.

"Does that make sense?" he asks.

The giddiness in my heart breaks loose and I let out a little laugh. "I've felt that way about you for years."

He smiles. "Really?"

"I don't know how I feel about it being a new experience for <u>you</u>," I tease.

He smiles and kisses me then, embracing me firmly. I kiss him back and we hold onto each other with relief.

I pull back and he puts his hand on my cheek.

"Come on," he says. "Let's go home."

Chapter 22

Two months later, Erik's mom is home and mostly recovered from surgery. After seeing how Erik's handled the results of the Hess Competition, she's softened her approach towards me and been more supportive in general. We've even discovered we have something in common: a mutual love of Nutter Butters. It's not much, but it's a start.

Meanwhile, our careers have taken a turn no one could have anticipated, thanks to the meddling of Sam and Jack.

I had forgotten all about the video Sam took of me and Erik playing together at the Rivers Paradise Resort, but she didn't forget. After a bit of plotting and scheming, Sam and Jack convinced Chloe and Grayson to post the video to their YouTube channel.

Five days and half a million hits later, they let us in on the secret.

Chloe was afraid we'd be mad, but after seeing so many views, along with comments like "captivating" and "I couldn't look away," why would we be? In fact, at that point, Erik and I started to envision something new.

Grayson and Chloe helped us start a channel of our own, and he helped us get some recording equipment set up so we could make more videos of our collaborations. We've posted clips of us playing individually, too. Our new videos have even more hits than the first, which suits me fine since the sound-quality of Sam's "perfectly fine" phone video kind of sucked.

In the avalanche of emails we've received since then, we've secured one of the best managers in the industry and he's currently arranging a ten-stop national tour that will culminate at none other than Lincoln Center.

But for now, Erik and I are enjoying a moment of solitude and normalcy. We're walking along our old stretch of the

353

Greenbelt, hand in hand. He's come home with me to Boise and managed to reconcile with my parents. Before we left the house, my dad even pulled me aside and told me how nice it is to have Erik be part of the family again.

We approach my favorite bridge and draw to a stop at the top. The river dances below, and the trees rustle lightly as the spring breeze plays through. We lean on the rail, arms touching elbow to shoulder. I can't help but smile.

I look over at him, the boy I loved who grew into the man I love even more. I nudge him slightly with my hip. He smiles, leans in, and kisses me oh so gently. My heart flutters around in my chest. We pull apart, looking at one another and staying close. What a journey it's been with Erik so far.

Unless I'm wrong, I have a feeling we've only just begun.

The End

About the Author

Jordyn White writes steamy romances featuring smart, sexy women and the swoon-worthy men who adore them. Her sexy love stories are full of passion but don't skimp on the tenderness. She's addicted to trendy coffee houses, poolside lounging, and HEAs. When not tapping blissfully away on her laptop, she takes time to enjoy life with her husband and their children.

JordynWhiteBooks.com

Printed in April 2019
by Rotomail Italia S.p.A., Vignate (MI) - Italy